C000155746

THE MUSIC BOX

by

Howard G. Awbery

An environmentally friendly book printed and bound in England by
www.printondemand-worldwide.com

Mixed Sources
Product group from well-managed
forests, and other controlled sources
www.fsc.org Cert no. TT-COC-002641
© 1996 Forest Stewardship Council
FSC

PEFC Certified
This product is
from sustainably
managed forests
and controlled
sources
www.pefc.org
PEFC
PEFC/16-33-415

This book is made entirely of chain-of-custody materials

Howard G. Awbery

Cover designed by James Bucklow

To all my past friends, my present friends and friends that I have yet to meet...

Characters in The Music Box are not based on any real life people, either alive or dead, and any similarity is coincidental.

www.fast-print.net/store.php

THE MUSIC BOX

Copyright © Howard G Awbery 2014

All rights reserved

No part of this book may be reproduced in any form by photocopying
or any electronic or mechanical means, including information storage
or retrieval systems, without permission in writing from both the
copyright owner and the publisher of the book.

The right of Howard G Awbery to be identified as the author of this work
has been asserted by him in accordance with the Copyright, Designs and
Patents Act 1988 and any subsequent amendments thereto.

A catalogue record for this book is available from the British Library

ISBN 978-178456-150-5

First published 2014 by
FASTPRINT PUBLISHING
Peterborough, England.

1
King's Cross-Station, London

The overnight steam engine to Scotland snorted like a stallion before a race. The whoosh and hiss of excessive pressure drove clouds of steam billowing from between its wheels. The noise hastened passengers to embark. It also encouraged those not travelling to rapidly disembark or join their loved ones on the overnight journey.

Platform 7, King's Cross Station rang to the sound of carriage doors being slammed shut. Passengers waved through smoke-smutted windows and lovers leant perilously out of the sash windows of the doors savouring their last, lingering, gymnastic kisses. The smell from a railway steam engine mixed with sulphur from the coal is a smell like no other smell. It lingers in the memory from excited childhood through to adulthood. But today the steam smelt differently. It smelt of urgency. It smelt of challenge and every second delay increased its irritation.

Suddenly, heads turned all along the platform as a cacophony of excitement attracted their attention. A jamboree of laughter and noise preceded 20 revellers tumbling out of snow-covered taxis onto King's Cross Station. The carousers were obviously a wedding party who shouted and waved to hold the limbering train as they started to run along the platform towards the last carriage door remaining open.

The wedding party's original plan, following a lavish and very 'wet' wedding breakfast, was to wave the happy couple off at the station in a leisurely fashion - a plan completely thwarted by London's unpredictable weather conditions. Snow had brought London to a virtual standstill; travel was almost impossible. Huge financial inducements had been necessary to secure enough taxis for the whole wedding group to travel to the station; further, even greater financial inducements had been required to get the happy couple to the station in time to catch the train.

Hand in hand, laughing uncontrollably and running at the front of the melee were the newlyweds followed by a cloud of spent confetti and rice. The groom held onto his trilby as he ran, his gabardine raincoat and belt flowing like a cape behind. The bride, running as fast as the inappropriate footwear of her going-away-outfit would allow, laughed and waved her scarf frantically with her free hand. Behind them followed a crowd of mixed ages and running ability. Athletic friends of the bride and groom flanked the couple like wingmen, followed by puffing aunts and portly uncles. Perched Boadicea-like, on top of the newlywed's cases, on a heavy porter's trolley sat an elderly gentleman waving his walking stick, goading two puffing younger guests to push him faster to catch up with the fray.

The carnival of noise was carefully funnelled towards the only open carriage door by amused platform staff and the two, young, apologetic travellers unceremoniously ushered up the steep carriage steps. Their embarkation was accelerated by stern looks flashed by the Station Master, whose face swapped from obvious irritation to sickly courtesy and back again in an instant. He kept glancing at his silver fob watch, which appeared welded to his right palm, its lid permanently open.

As soon as the couple were safely on board, the heavy porter's trolley, cases and elderly passenger were threaded through the happy group to the front. The gentleman, an image of the groom but 30 years his senior, was helped off the cases by his two, young, puffing guests. They continued to hold him, as they led him to the carriage, steadying his wedding breakfast lubricated legs. Leaning forward through the open carriage door, the elderly gentleman kissed and hugged his new daughter-in-law. He then closed both hands tightly around the hand of the groom as if not accepting or wanting to let him go, even now, saying with wet eyes: "I'm so proud of you son and, well...

you know, your mother... well she'd have been, well... you know, don't you?"

The emotional family scene was rudely interrupted by loud coughing from the watch-obsessed Station Master and the cases bundled unceremoniously in through the open door which was immediately slammed shut. The Station Master nodded vigorously at the platform guard whose shrill whistle slipped the imaginary tether off the snorting engine and the piqued steed lurched forward, noisily taking up the slack between the carriages.

The revellers at first, were able to walk alongside the slowly accelerating carriages blowing kisses and shouting their good wishes to the newlyweds but gradually fell behind as the train gathered momentum. Calls from the revellers of 'good luck' and 'congratulations' drowned out the competition and a huge cheer went up as the bride's bouquet of cornflower colours flew out through the open sash window. The symbolic scrabble for the bouquet was won by the elderly gentleman who smiling, passed it on to the youngest and most timid bridesmaid.

Shrinking as it snaked out of King's Cross Station, the train began its long journey to Scotland. Once outside the station, the train clattered over the confusing myriad of criss-crossing points to a bumpy rhythm, each carriage experiencing the jolts from the rail joints a few seconds later than the previous carriage. Once free of the points, the night train to Scotland gathered speed by the yard.

When the last carriage had disappeared out of site, the revellers turned and headed for the station exit. The elderly gentleman climbed back onto the porter's trolley only to be told by the two, still wheezing young wedding guests that anyone who can beat four young bridesmaids to a flying bouquet could walk!

Back inside the jolting vestibule of the carriage, the newlyweds brushed snow from each other's coats. Some of the flakes had melted on the bride's blue beret and the drops sparkled in the smoke-yellowed, corridor lights. The groom dabbed a droplet on the beret with his fingertip and planted it on the tip of his bride's smiling nose. She stretched up on to her tiptoes, dreamily closed her eyes to kiss her new husband when they were abruptly joined by a short, sprightly butler who introduced himself courteously as Albert Jennings. He announced with rehearsed flourish that he would be looking after them for the duration of their journey.

Albert pulled hard on the wide leather strap that secured the sash window in the carriage door and it shut with a bang, leaving behind the snow-covered world outside the accelerating train. In the now silent vestibule he automatically rubbed the steamed up window with his blue and gold uniform sleeve and peered out into the black:

"Not sure we should be going anywhere tonight sir. Station Master should've cancelled this trip in my view. But that's just my view. Who am I? I've just been travelling this line for 16 years. Nobody takes any notice of me sir."

"Gets far worse as we go further north they says. The York crew, who just arrived in London, says the track will be albeit impassable any further north than York. You young people chose the worst night I can ever remember to travel. Mark my words we're in for a hell of a journey tonight. Please follow me."

Carston looked at Celia and, behind Albert's back so he couldn't see, shot his eyes skyward, silently mouthing, 'probably didn't finish the positivity course'. Celia dug him in the ribs mouthing, 'behave'.

Albert Jennings proceeded to noisily bump and scrape the newlywed's brand new leather cases against every door and pillar along the corridor to their compartment. Dutifully, he opened the sliding door and gestured for them to go through first. When all three, including the cases, were squashed inside the tiny compartment, Albert mechanically recited: "Dinner is at 8.00 pm and served in the restaurant car. The restaurant car is three carriages towards the front of the train. Excuse me for saying sir, but most gentlemen dress for dinner." Carston unconsciously smoothed the creases in his shabby raincoat trying to ignore the slight. With that, Albert turned and coughed gently into his hand, waiting patiently.

"Oh, yes. Yes of course," said Carston with some embarrassment and pulled out his wallet. He searched for a 10 shilling note, found none and ended up reluctantly handing Albert a £1 note. Albert gently slid the compartment door shut.

Before anyone else could interrupt them again, the exhausted newlyweds finally kissed. She relaxed into his arms and for the very first time they both felt they had come home. On parting, Celia said: "Fancy your father getting so drunk he had to be wheeled down the platform on a porter's trolley." She laughed as she said it, there being no scorn whatsoever in her voice. She had become very fond of the lovely old gentleman in the short time she had known him.

"Always does it," mused Carston, "every wedding, as long as I can remember. Drunk as a lord. He was quite well behaved this time. Sometimes he ends up being brought home by the constabulary. He always says, 'if I can't get drunk at my son, or cousin, or a friend's wedding then when in the world can I get drunk?'

They both laughed as they took off their steaming outer clothes and hung them on the polished brass hooks near the door into the corridor.

For the first time they acknowledged the cramped compartment, remarking about the same, familiar, dusty, musty, train smell that pervaded every compartment on every train either had ever travelled; that dry, dusty, carpet smell from the brocades and heavily upholstered seats.

Carston suggested that as well as the smell of the compartment soft furnishings, every traveller left a trace of themselves long after their journey; their cologne, their personal sweat, their cigar or pipe smoke. Added to the fact that everyone loses ten pounds of skin a year of which there was probably an accumulation inches deep on the floor!

Celia, horrified at the thought, quickly stepped backwards examining the dark floor.

What she could smell as well as the soft furnishings, he suggested half in jest and half in his naturally serious self, was a cocktail of carriage smells mixed with people smells of all those passengers who had ever travelled in their compartment. Celia reeved her nose up dismissing his theory out of hand saying: "I would prefer not to think of anyone else ever using 'our wedding compartment, thank you very much!"
Carston laughed at the romantic thought of it being, 'their wedding compartment' and continued busying himself with a thorough examination of the tiny corner washbasin and the clever engineering of the mechanism that raised and lowered the upper bunk bed.

Celia squeezed past Carston to rub the steamed outer window and sat watching the pattern of big white flakes fly horizontally past the window as the train sped through the darkness. Minutes passed before she touched his sleeve to attract his attention saying: "Darling, the snow really does look very heavy. Perhaps the butler was right." A level of anxiety edged her voice.

Carston pooh-poohed her concern saying: "These train drivers see it as a challenge. They're true professionals. They can drive these engines blindfolded. They live and breathe them. They dream about steam engines when they lay alongside their wives in bed. If it was a choice of sleep with a beautiful woman or stand on the footplate of The Royal Scot, The Royal Scot would win every time.

"These drivers dream of engines from the past and replay, in their mind's eye, memorable journeys they've travelled. On a serious note they also know when the weather is so bad they have to say 'not today'."

As an afterthought he laughed saying: "Anyway, we can't get lost can we? We're on rails all the way to Scotland. It's not as though we're going to end up at Aberystwyth or Taunton or in the middle of a field is it?"

Celia smiled, patted the hard seat next to her and shuffled along making room for him. Carston joined her and the two of them huddled closely together on the forward facing seat watching the hypnotic, flying snow mixed with steam and smoke.

She shared with him that, as it was her wedding day, she would see the snow, not as a cold, wet problem but as bright, white confetti arranged especially for them by their amazingly romantic train company. She laughed as she demonstrated the engine driver and fireman throwing handfuls of confetti up into the air to drift back over their carriage. Carston's eyes looked skyward at her vivid imagination.

She snuggled into him for warmth and wrapped his arm more tightly around her as they talked and laughed about incidents that had occurred at the wedding breakfast, in particular, the sauciness of the best man's speech. They tried to guess who had eaten most of the wedding cake and decided it had been his father with his aunt coming a close second. They both acknowledged how lucky they had been to get enough taxis to get them all to the station. They laughed at how grumpy the Station Master had been when they were late and Celia mimicked his sonorous tone whilst looking up and down at her hand and a pretend fob-watch.

Suddenly, there was a knock at the door. Celia quickly untangled herself from him and sat up straight as though her mother had caught them kissing in her parents' front parlour. Carston laughed: "It's OK Mrs Prestwick, we are married."

Nevertheless, Celia brushed her hair back, smoothed her dress over her knees, folded her hands in her lap and sat primly. The door slid open slowly. It was Albert again; this time he was carrying a silver tray upon which stood two champagne flutes and a bottle of Moet & Chandon.

"Compliments of the Restaurant Manager sir. We do it for all the newlyweds and seeing all the confetti I'm going to have to clean up in here I think I'm probably right. Congratulations from all of the staff on the overnight express to Scotland."

"How lovely," declared Celia as she jumped up and relieved him of the tray.

"Yes splendid," repeated Carston touched by the gesture but already feeling the poorer.

A cough from Albert again unlocked the wallet and Carston now faced another dilemma. If he gave Albert £1 for carrying the suitcases 10 yards, then how much should he give him for a bottle of good champagne delivered to his compartment? £5 was reluctantly handed over and a delighted Albert left, saying he hoped they enjoy the champagne and, in parting, explained that he would transform their carriage whilst they were enjoying dinner, ready for them turning in for the night.

2 Early Years

The groom, Carston L.G. Prestwick, left school at 18 vowing never, ever to go to university. He had seen his older brother party and drink his way through three wasted years of his life using the age-old excuses, 'it was always Freshers' Week'. He dressed like a scruffy student, lived like a scruffy student and eventually left university as a scruffy student with a scraped 2:2. He ended up working in the City of London for an uncle, in a job he hated. Carston was uninspired by his idle brother's choice of routes to the future.

However, Providence has a habit of ignoring man's best laid plans and having started an engineering apprenticeship with Rosser's Steam Engine Manufacturing Company Ltd based in Leeds, Carston was immediately identified as having 'talent' and fast tracked into Brunel University, the best engineering university in London. He emerged five hard years later, with a PhD in physics.

Carston was not the archetypal boffin, forever sporting an elbow patched, weekend cardigan, pock marked down the front by smoker's burn holes, complete with stretched pockets for pipe and matches, frayed shirt collars, thick glasses and no social life. Neither was he at the other end of the scale, a member of the tweed, three-piece suit brigade, shod in Brogues, always at parties, having canapés on the lawn and forever taking re-sits. On the contrary, he cleverly positioned himself somewhere between. Having finally decided to go to university he decided he would balance the partying with some serious studying. His sacrosanct study schedule could not be broken however hard his fellow flat mates tried. He was quite happy for them to party all night and day never complaining. They, in turn, knew that when Carston decided to party then they could be in for a marathon. A comment best describing Carston came from a friend who had, 'spent a week drinking with him one night'.

Throughout his time at university a plethora of girls followed in Carston's wake, each watching and waiting for the current belle to put a foot wrong, each dreaming of threading their arm through the arm of the best looking man on campus, aisle-bound.

As the antithesis of his brother, Carston wore fashionable clothes, holidayed in the south of France in the summer, skied in Wengen in the winter and was in love with the brutal engineering of his open topped sports car. Early on he had become part of the engineering academic elite, specialising in steam locomotion power and privileged to be invited to join certain engineering organisations whose membership was preserved for, 'the more mature candidate'.

Having lost his mother when he was 10 he was raised by his very competitive father and, to some extent, his bone-idle brother. Slowing down or reducing his effort in anything, whether it be school work or sport, always resulted in his father's words loudly ringing in his ears: 'Remember son, it's only the lead Husky who has the best view.' The imagery portrayed always made him smile but drove him on. His home life had been uneventful save for his father's repeated request: 'when you finish playing with trains come and join me in Chambers.'

'Not a chance,' repeated Carston just as often. 'And when you've finished dressing up in wigs and tights and fur robes you can come and be my fire-man.'

Carston's PhD was entitled, 'An Investigation into the Effects of Locomotive Engine Smoke on the Forward Visibility of Drivers'. His research had been directed by his university tutor following the fateful outcome of a spate of accidents that had occurred in 1937 where, because of poor visibility caused by engine smoke, a number of locomotives across the country had crashed into stationary sets of carriages, injuring many passengers.

Carston's research led him in many directions, but what fascinated him most was the work of the French steam engineer Andre Chapelon and the Finnish engineer Kyost Kylala. Between them, they had invented the 'KylChap double blast pipes'. These KylChap blast pipes deflected the smoke upwards at a significantly accelerated speed, hence dispersing the smoke more effectively preventing it from obscuring the visibility of the cab of the locomotive. The driver's visibility had been considerably improved by the KylChap invention and the new device was already being widely installed in France.

However, what Carston also secretly discovered was that, with slight modifications to their invention, not only could he significantly improve driver visibility, he could increase the performance of the locomotive by a staggering 19%. So sensitive was his discovery that he was immediately withdrawn from normal duties with Rosser's and moved, by The Department of Internal Affairs in the British Government, to work at a secret set of railway sidings terminating in their own, heavily guarded locomotive sheds. These locomotive sheds were located near South Ruislip, just outside West London. He was made to sign the Official Secrets Act, given a Doncaster Works-built A3 class locomotive 2751 and an engineering team. However, any trials on the locomotive could only be conducted at night and under armed guards. The livery of the locomotive had been changed, as was the unique locomotive number and name, such was the sensitivity of the time.

In 1938, with the onset of war imminent, an increase in the performance of steam locomotives of 19% would have an immensely positive impact on the war effort. The speed of transport would be increased, the payload could be raised significantly, but the most important impact would be the reduction in the quantity of coal required; coal that was so desperately needed all over the country in preparation for war.

Rosser Steam Engine Manufacturing Company Ltd were not happy about one of their leading steam engineers being taken to work on a secret project, but came to a compromise with the British Government. Carston would work full time at the secret location but he would be released to participate in the prestigious north/south, steam, speed trial, taking place on 30th April 1938. The second compromise was Carston could use any modification he was working on in the race on behalf of Rosser's.

The north/south speed trial had run informally for many years but no longer was it considered a fun event, it had become serious, very serious. Each competitor company would use an, as yet undisclosed, locomotive of their choice, accompanied by seven coaches on the East Coast Main Line near Stoke Bank - the official UK steam speed trial site. The prestige of winning the speed trial a third time in a row would be immense for Rosser's, but for any of the other contestants the value of winning for the first time would be immeasurable. It would stand the winning company head and shoulders above all the railway competition and attract huge investment. The stakes had become very high.

Rosser's main rival was the Westerman Railway co., a railway company backed by huge sums of money and with an aggressive reputation for winning. For the last two years Rosser's had won the speed title much to the chagrin of Westerman's MD. They had done so by the superiority of their engineering and were once again in with a chance.

Carston's research findings would give Rosser's the edge over all the competition in the UK and investors would fall over each other to be associated with such success. Rosser's new Chairman, Nigel Rosser, dreamt of winning the race again and adding an international steam speed record, to boot.

Nigel Rosser, by default, had abruptly taken over the reins of the company from his father. His father had been a strange beast in the cutthroat world of steam, equally respected and feared. He was a social hearted man with a business head and part-time Baptist minister. His staff were his family and he looked after them as if they were his own. At the age of 70 years, Nigel's father enjoyed nothing more than to don a blue boiler suit and his greasy cap and join the footplate men for a day. It was there he met his end. A massive heart attack killed him instantly doing the job he loved; in the place he loved to be with the friends he loved the most in the entire world.

Carston Prestwick's father was delighted with his son's academic performance and insisted upon celebrating fully with his son and attending the graduation ceremony in London. Carston complied dutifully and had dinner with the proud new Chairman of Rosser's, Nigel Rosser and Carston's father the night prior to the graduation ceremony. The ceremony was followed by a celebration lunch with his tutors, the dean and the pro-vice chancellor again with his father. He didn't even flinch when his father stood up and clapped at the ceremony when Dr Carston Prestwick 'trod the boards'. But secretly Carston couldn't wait for the evening party and celebrations culminating in a joint London Universities Graduation Ball.

Completely single for the first time in ages, he had promised himself not to become attached again but just enjoy life. He didn't want the commitment; he didn't want the endless questions about what he was working on. It didn't matter how often he explained he couldn't say because of the Official Secrets Act, the women in his life seemed to see it as a personal challenge to tease a secret out of him, by fair means or womanly guile. They wanted some snippet that only they would be privileged to know. The Official Secrets Act was like a magnet to some women and a sexual turn on to others. At first the secrecy and intrigue had been fun, but it soon became tedious not being able to be certain why some women were attracted to him.

Then he met Celia.

Celia, the bride, had experienced a completely different childhood. It was expected that she would leave Fort William Grammar School for Girls at 17, just as her parents wanted. It was expected she would go to Secretarial College and become a typist in a typing pool at one of the many shipyards in Scotland, just as her parents wanted. A very good job, 'for a woman,' her old-fashioned father repeatedly reminded her, reinforcing his advice by pointing knowledgably at her from his chair with his soot-encrusted, teeth-scored, smoking, briar pipe.

However, once again, Providence steered a completely different path for her. In the 4th year of school Celia fell madly in love with a boy called Austin McGregor, but from afar. Austin McGregor attended the Fort William Grammar School for Boys but as there were insufficient numbers of pupils for certain subjects, both schools shared teachers. Celia was absolutely besotted with Austin, a tall, popular, good-looking boy with a mop of dark, curly hair. Austin McGregor was good at everything, sport, exams, socially and in love. Like a magnet, he attracted the prettiest girls in the 5th year, the lower 6th year and even some of the upper 6th year. Austin hardly spoke to 'Specky-four-eyes' as Celia was better known to some of her bitchy 'friends'.

So besotted had she been that she had secretly stolen his school scarf and slept every night with it under her pillow. She could smell him on the scarf and wrapped it around herself to dream whenever she was alone in her room. It was her only link with him for he seemed never to even give her a second glance.

Celia decided that the only way to attract any attention from Austin was to out-shine him because he was so competitive. Coming second to her would really make him sit up and take notice. Now, sport was not an option because girls and boys were segregated for games. Socially she couldn't compete for he really was charming, but in exams she thought she might just have a chance. Celia's head went down in the 4th form and didn't rise up again until she matriculated in the 6th form with the highest results in either of the Fort William Grammar School histories.

Her marks won her the coveted scholarship to university without which, further full-time education would have been impossible. Even Austin congratulated her, making her knees go weak. As only a very small number of students had matriculated with sufficiently high marks to go to university the cluster, which included Celia and Austin, was small. They sat closely together in the common room discussing their options excitedly, nominating their first and second choices of university. Celia had achieved her first objective and was now in a very small group of friends with Austin and highly regarded by him. Having now become one of his friends Celia was absolutely over the moon when she and Austin were both accepted at the same London medical university. Her plans were unfolding nicely. Now they would get closer both being freshers, now they would find their way around London together, they would stay in the same halls of residence for first year students, perhaps they might even share a house together in the second year and third year, but that was a dream too far ahead to contemplate. Nevertheless Celia did dream.

Two weeks before they planned to leave Fort William to go to university, Austin declared he was going to have a gap year and travel!

Celia was devastated. This was not the plan. How could he do this? She had reduced the number of competitors for his affections down from the total number of 5th, lower 6th and upper 6th form girls in Fort William Grammar School for Girls, to just a small group of girls with high exam results and then again she had reduced the competition down to just the two of them going to the same university in London. She imagined they would travel together; they would make new friends together and who knew where it might end.

Austin McGregor going travelling on his own was not part of her plan!

She had to make a decision. 'Her' Austin had been her inspiration and drive for success. Draped in his school scarf he had been the reason she had toiled day and night when all of her friends were out partying. For that she would be ever grateful to him. But him going away was not how it was supposed to be. It wasn't fair. At night she beat her pillow in frustration and cried herself to sleep night after night. Her decision, after much deliberation, and finding out that her scholarship would not be held over for another year, was to go to university on her own and find another 'Austin McGregor'.

Her area of study was paediatrics, specialising in paediatric speech therapy. She had seen the results on some of the local school children with learning disabilities and was so impressed by the patience and determination of the therapists that her pathway was clear. Finally, settling in London at university, Celia centred her whole life on children. She attended performances of children with speech difficulties from the local schools. She walked around paediatric ENT wards in hospitals on her weekends off; she bought heaps of raffle tickets for prizes she didn't want.

After four years of study she attained a first class honours degree in Paediatric Speech Therapy. She was immediately headhunted for a position at Great Ormond Street Hospital and started work before she even had time for a holiday.

Her parents were so proud of her but, being elderly and uncomfortable travelling the long journey from Scotland to London, were unable to see her graduate, much to her sadness. But she did manage to go to the joint London Universities Graduation Ball.

3
King's Cross Station, Canteen

George Unwin the train driver and Percy Brown the fireman sat in the canteen in their blue faded boiler suits and loose jackets listening intently. They were listening to the BBC weather report coming from the wireless balanced upon a shelf in King's Cross Station's canteen before their shift. As footplate-man and fireman of the overnight train to Scotland, the weather report was their Bible and with the forecasted snow and wind already across London they were keen to hear the reports about the rest of the country.

The canteen was a smoke-filled haven for railway workers. It smelled of steak and kidney pie and freshly cooked chips, of roly-poly pudding and apple crumble. It was a safe place to be, no fancy airs and graces, just solid home-cooked food for solid working folk who ate dinner at lunchtime and supper early in the evening.

All the staff of the night train to Scotland, consisting of the footplate man and fireman, restaurant staff, train guard, butlers and cabin staff, had a vested interest in the decision-making process of whether or not the train would be cancelled due to the bad weather. Either they would all be sent home, or they would be off to Scotland. They also knew that the most vociferous arguers were not always the key decision makers. Things were looking good for a very early finish on full pay and nobody wanted to jeopardise the decision. Even the banter from the platform porters was unusually tempered, all of them understood the decision hinged on the weather report. The canteen was ominously quiet. Plates weren't moved, cutlery wasn't sorted and the banter at the till was hushed.

The BBC weather reporter continued his expressionless presentation: "Snow on high ground would move south and before dawn there would be wide-spread coverage. Several inches could be expected by morning as far south as London following a line to the East of the Pennines. Some drifting had been reported in exposed areas. High winds would further exacerbate disruption to transport in the centre of the country and car drivers are advised, that unless their journey was absolutely necessary, to avoid travelling."

The ultimate decision for the train to travel or be cancelled lay with the portly Station Master who scowled at the best of times and now was not the best of times.

"What say you, George?" the Station Master asked of the more senior of the two footplate-men.

"Could always pull off at York if it gets too bad," said George, "what do you think Percy?"

An explosion followed: "It's barmy, madness, going out in this weather. It's snowing like 'ell out there. What more do you need than the BBC, the actual BBC, not some piddly local radio station, the actual BBC, telling you 'not to go out unless your journey is absolutely necessary'. But I don't suppose anyone will listen to me I'm just in the cab. The company's more interested in profits than our safety." And with that he slumped down cradling his huge, steaming mug of sweet tea and disappeared into his own grumpy, Scottish, Unionist world.

George and Percy had worked the big A3 series locomotives together for about 20 years. George, the train driver, was the shorter and slighter man in his early 50s who praised loudly and blamed softly. His thin, greying hair showed beneath his regulation peaked train driver's cap; a regulation cap he would wear until they were on the footplate then off it would come to be replaced by his old, worn leather one. The regulation cap would be returned as they drew into their destination station. George had been offered a more senior position within the company but the thought of not standing on the footplate of a loco filled him with dread. He was very experienced and been chosen by Rosser's as driver for the illustrious 1936 and 1937 steam time trials; probably the most prestigious position to which any locomotive driver could ever aspire.

Percy on the other hand was a fiery Scot as were many firemen. He stood 6ft 2ins tall and worked as hard as any man George had ever come across. Percy could throw shovelfuls of coal from the back of the tender into the firebox without so much as a cobble spilling onto the footplate. George didn't know all Percy's history but believed he could probably drive the locomotive himself if ever it was necessary. There were gaps in his history that George chose not to investigate.

Percy's distinguishing feature was that he had no front teeth so everything he said included a whistle. Accompanied by his Glaswegian accent few knew what he was saying except, that is George after 20 years. But not even George knew the full story behind his missing teeth. What he did know was that there was a pub in Glasgow somewhere where Percy had been on a 'bender' many years before. Having run out of money, he left his teeth behind the bar as collateral for the night's drinking. Sadly, Percy to this day had not been able to remember which pub.

George and Percy knew how each other thought and never had a seriously cross word. Today would be no different. Once decided, George knew Percy would be 100% with him whatever the decision. He was completely dependable.

However, George acknowledged this weather was worse than any they had ever travelled in before.

The Station Master went over to the window, rubbed the steamed glass with his sleeve, looked out and declared more as a wish than a fact: "It seems to be easing a bit."

Percy followed him and looked out of the same window: "Easing my arse!!! Flakes as big as golf balls and settling too. Looks like Switzerland out there. Eskimo Nell wouldn't go out in this." The station staff and all the train staff laughed. The Station Master glowered.

George took a look and suggested: "Why not ring York and see what it's like there, then make the decision?" A rumble of agreement came from the rest of the railwaymen.

The Station Master left the canteen and went to his office, George followed. Inside the dusty office the Station Master shared his concerns with George.

"See, the trouble is George, we have this big wig getting married and travelling to Scotland for his honeymoon. Normally, big wigs don't impress me but this Doctor Carston Pringle works for Rosser's and is very high up. It's rumoured he's in line to be the company's next engineering chief." This being the

Station Master's criteria as whether to risk the safety of the train by travelling on such a bad night did not impress George one bit and his silence said it all.

The Station Master noted George's disdain, " OK, OK, OK, I'll call York."

After the call he put the receiver down and looked straight at George: "Well it's better than I expected. They say there's a sprinkling of snow, about an inch settled around the station at the moment but it's stopped snowing now. Then hesitantly he added, "however, there is a fair bit of wind about."

George looked doubtfully at the Station Master.
"Ring them yourself if you don't believe me," he challenged.

George ignored the comment and went back into the canteen, gathered up his ex-army, khaki lunch bag and said: "Come on Percy, we're going to Scotland."
The whole train crew groaned in unison as they rose.

"Bonkers, we must all be barmy. We don't need the bloody BBC to tell us it's snowing. We can see it's snowing. We can 'all' see it's snowing. That is all of us other than the blind Station Master. What did York say?" asked Percy, dutifully following George out of the homely kitchen canteen and onto the platform with its biting wind and promise of a wild night. They walked along the platform in front of a straggle of reluctant staff.

"A sprinkling of snow with some wind."

"And if you believe that then I'm the tooth fairy."

George laughed and eventually, so did Percy.

They climbed up onto the footplate as they had done a thousand times before and set about their pre-journey checks.

The coal was at maximum height, the water tank was full and there were no obstructions in the tiny tender passage that led from the engine back to the carriages. The platform staff had done a good job of preparing the locomotive and the steam was virtually at driving pressure. George blew a blast of steam to clear the pipes through the system and smiled at the powerful whoosh and hiss.

They were ready to go.

4
Westerman's Board Room

Major Nicholas Brown stubbed out his fat, Havana cigar in the dustbin-lid sized crystal ashtray positioned in the centre of the acre of leather-covered boardroom table.

The pipe and cigar smoke in the room layered down thick and heavy from the ornate ceiling, reflecting the meeting's mood.

Scowling from the four dark walls were the portraits of previous company Chairmen. Whiskered, stern, standing or sitting in judgement, all posing to emphasise their importance in the history of the Westerman Railway Company. With ramrod-straight backs exaggerating their integrity and upright citizenship. they listened to every word that went on in the boardroom from their lofty pulpits. When the current FD, once again, announced the poor financial position of the company, Major Brown could almost hear the pictures tut-tutting their disapproval. The worst criticism came from the founder. A short, blustering, burly man who, reportedly started the railway company with just a wheelbarrow and shovel. Major Brown tried to blank out their piercing stares but inwardly knew they were right in their judgement. This was the third loss-making year and the situation was unsustainable. He could also feel the cold breath and wolverine teeth of the shareholders closing in on, what they would see as, a sacrificial chairman.

His last trip to generate investment from the Continent had taken longer than expected and had been significantly more stressful than he imagined. Europe was in turmoil and nobody was investing in anything other than armaments. Even the normally buoyant Swiss banking world had come to a standstill and he had heard the same excuse from all quarters, 'come back when the war is over.' He had returned to Westerman's to continually falling profits, reduced passenger numbers and a reluctance for anyone to grasp the situation and do something about it. The only way out of the situation was to win the forthcoming steam speed race and restore him into favour with the shareholders. Win by whatever means necessary.

He growled a series of questions at the board room full of mainly obese corporate mandarins: "Who the hell is this Doctor Carston bloody Prestwick anyway? And why didn't we get to him before the competition?

And why is he locked away in the Government's South Ruislip works? And what's he working on?"

The five, suited, board members shuffled uneasily at the machine-gunning of questions. They had no answers and to be answerless in the Chairman's office was tantamount to lining up and moving your head slowly across a butcher's block, one after the other, waiting for the butcher's heavy cleaver to fall.

It fell.

"Richardson," snapped Major Brown, pointing at him with his glowing cigar and leaving a trail of ash across the table. "Tell me why, in God's name, you didn't spot this brainbox when he was still at university? You're supposed to be in bloody personnel aren't you? How come we recruit a bunch of idiots who don't know the difference between conjugated valve gears and a bloody egg whisk and you let a man like Prestwick slip through? Eh, eh, eh?"

The four other mandarins tried to become invisible in their seats avoiding eye contact or any chance of deflecting the tirade onto themselves. They regularly joked, out of earshot, that the Major's meetings could be likened to 'playing leapfrog with a unicorn'.

Richardson shuffled uneasily on his seat. He had a decision to make. Offer a series of excuses that would summarily be minced up by the Chairman and spat out or, take his chances and say nothing. He settled on the latter.

His decision was rewarded by a deflection.

"Shawcross, what's this Prestwick working on?"

Shawcross, as Director of Engineering, had worked for the company for 30 years under four different chairmen and Major Brown was the one he feared the most. The others had been gentlemen; never raising their voices, but this man was an animal. Possibly suited for warfare but not for the science of railway engineering or corporate life.

Shawcross mumbled a reply: "It is thought sir, Dr Prestwick is working on a form of smoke deflection to improve visibility for footplate-men. An area he studied at university, I'm reliably informed sir."

"By whom is it thought he is working on smoke?" mimicked Major Brown "and if he is working on smoke then why the hell is he undertaking trials at night on a guarded train from a secret location, pray? Have you read his dissertation?" the questions increased in volume.

"No sir. It is understood, sir, that his dissertation has been withdrawn from the university library shelves as it contains information sensitive to the nation's security."

"That's the exact reason why we bloody well need to read it!" yelled Major Brown, his face reddening by the second.

"Get out, all of you. It's like working with the bloody Mothers' Union getting anything done around here. And Richardson, if you can't find any talent that's up and coming, your successor will!"

Richardson gunshot flinched as he left the boardroom.

Major Brown sat down heavily in his leather clad, high-backed, carver chair and snapped: "Not you Pickard."

Pickard, the company's Head of Security, returned to his seat. Pickard had spent 10 years in the armed forces and was the only board member with whom Major Brown felt he could relate.

Lighting yet another cigar, Major Brown spoke through the smoke cloud:

"What's your take on this?"

"Well sir, I don't think for one moment he is just working on visibility! I think, for it to be so secret, it must have a greater national significance. It must be something else. I think we should start by trying to retrieve Prestwick's dissertation. It shouldn't be so hard. We should be able to get past university security staff easily enough. His dissertation must be in some back office somewhere. After that we ought to get a look inside the locomotive works at South Ruislip. Then it would be up to you sir."

Major Brown puffed on the cigar thoughtfully.

"Risks?"

"At the university it shouldn't be such a big deal. We could pay a student to lift the dissertation and, if caught, we know nothing about it. It would be part of the deal with the student. However, if we were caught at the South Ruislip works then that's a completely different matter. That would be a national security breach, lots of noise and finger pointing sir. Someone's head would have to roll."

Brown considered the statement for a full minute.

"Shawcross's?" Major Brown suggested.

"If that's what you want sir. It's a bit harsh on the old guy but he certainly would have motive of professional kudos and fear of losing his job. His career would be over and it would be a miracle if he wasn't locked up for years as a deterrent to others."

"Needs must," snapped Major Brown and after a long pause said: "Do it."

"I'll keep you informed sir." And with that, Pickard left a very thoughtful Major Brown's smoke-filled boardroom.

5
A London Antique Shop

In the dark, back room of a little London antique shop two men stood facing the desk. A short, bald, bespectacled man sat behind. The tallest standing man called Hans, respectfully replied: "Yes, of course sir," and left the back room followed by a small, subordinate weasel man in his wake. They slid out of the shop into the drizzly London night.

"Why in God's name did the courier put the music box out on the damn counter in the first place?"

"To pretend it wasn't all that important, to throw anyone watching off the scent?" offered the weasel man weakly.

"It certainly did that. Now it's up to us to get it back. Crass bloody stupidity, that's what I call it, crass bloody stupidity. It'll be a needle in a bloody haystack job."

The two, wet men slipped into a café, removed their dripping coats and trilby hats and hung the limp garments on the curly coat stand at the back of the shop. They ordered a tea and a coffee, sat in a corner and continued their conversation. Both spoke perfect English despite it not being their first language.

"So what do we know from your little chat with the stupid sales girl?" asked Hans of the weasel man.

"The woman who bought the music box was a nurse or someone who works in a hospital."

"Oh, that narrows it down," snapped Hans sarcastically.

"She's about to get married and it's a present for her husband-to-be," thoughtfully added the weasel man.

"So now all we have to do is find is a nurse who is about to get married. Oh, for God's sake, there are hundreds of nurses getting married. They are all frightened about the war. They all want to get married before the war starts so that if their new husbands don't come back they'll get a widow's pension."

"But this one is going to Scotland for her honeymoon."

"So now we have a nurse who is getting married and going to Scotland for her honeymoon. God this is like drawing teeth. I don't suppose she said when. The nurse could be there by now, she could be anywhere in the Highlands by now, shacked up in some croft and not coming out into daylight for two weeks. They may not even be getting married till bloody August."

Hans blew into his cup to cool down the thick coffee, then took out a pack of Gauloises cigarettes, pulled one out with his lips, lit it and sent the pungent smoke spiralling towards the ceiling. A long pause followed as the weasel man rummaged about in his memory to recall the conversation details with the sales girl.

"On Thursday, that's it. She's getting married on Thursday and going to Scotland on Thursday night on the overnight train from London," added the weasel man in triumph, remembering snippets of the conversation with the, less than bright, sales girl.

6
The Honeymoon Train Carriage

They linked arms in the traditional champagne way. Carston and Celia chinked glasses and with his spare arm he held her as close as the moving train would allow. Before he let her take a sip he asked: "Do you know what Dom Perignon said when he first invented champagne?" she shook her head. "He said, 'Come quickly everyone, I have just tasted the stars.'"

Carston looked deep into her pretty blue eyes and whispered: "Hello, Mrs Carston Prestwick," and gave her an affectionate squeeze and kissed her nose.

Celia replied: "And hello the newly married Dr Carston Prestwick."

Together they sipped the champagne and knew exactly what Dom Peringon meant. Together, on their honeymoon that night, they tasted the stars.

The empty champagne flutes were carefully placed upon the small, half-round table by the window. Then Carston lowered the three separate blinds to the corridor, locked the door and dimmed the compartment's yellow lights.

The carriage atmosphere was transformed into romance. True to her mother, Celia had not allowed any man to sleep with her until the day she wed. And here was her wedding day. Today had been her day and tonight was to be their night; here in a gently rocking railway carriage with the man she had fallen so deeply in love with, she couldn't believe her good fortune. They held each other watching the snow race past the window, drawing a white, lace curtain on the outside world.

Still standing and facing each other, Carston smoothed the fringe from her forehead and ran the back of his index finger down her cheek. When he reached her chin he stopped and tilted her face to be kissed. They kissed fleetingly then his finger continued its slow sensual journey downwards onto her neck following the contours of her slim throat until it stopped, caught in the v of the amber necklace he had given her as her wedding present. Celia smiled a thank you, leaned past him and lifted the lid of the ornate wooden musical box she had given to him as a wedding gift. She had searched everywhere to find something so special, eventually coming across it in a tiny antique shop tucked away in a London back street. She had known immediately that this was the present for him for it played Edelweiss, his favourite tune. Carston smiled.

He turned the necklace catching the dimly lit carriage light to highlight the million year old tiny encased insects in the rich yellow stone and then his finger continued tracing its path of anticipation down to the crease at the top of her cleavage. Celia's breath was coming in short bursts with the intimacy of his deliberate tender movements. She, in turn, started to undo his tie, slowly and deliberately provoking a shudder in him that transferred back to her in excitement that she had such power over him. Their movements quickened until they entered that wonderful, no-going-back, world that only lovers know.

And then everything disappeared for them. They heard nothing; they saw nothing and felt nothing other than a closeness neither had felt so powerfully before.

They made love to the clickety-clack of the locomotive wheels over the rail joints. They made love that evening slowly and tentatively, exploring each other's bodies and continually checking if their movements were all right, like strangers. They became one that evening in a railway carriage on the snowiest first night of their honeymoon, somewhere on their way to Fort William.

***

Whilst dressing for dinner in the cramped compartment they jostled each other playfully. Carston continually jogged her elbow as she tried to administer eyeliner and in retribution she tugged at the loose ends of his bow tie knowing it would infuriate the hell out of him. Eventually, when ready, they made their way to the restaurant car; she in a long, cream, lace dress and he in a dinner jacket. As they wove their way between the narrow tables the diners in turn looked up, smiled knowingly, raised their glasses and silently nodded their congratulations. Carston and Celia acknowledged each pair of diners with puzzled smiles.

At the newlywed's table a tell-tale sprinkling of confetti surrounded their plates. It explained how everybody in the restaurant knew they were newlyweds. They both laughed understanding. The diners close by smiled and raised their glasses a second time.

7
The Locomotive Cab

In the locomotive cab George put on his, non-regulation split screen motorcycle goggles, wrapped a scarf over his leather cap and tucked it tightly into his jacket. He peered out of the cab of the locomotive and looked ahead. Without the goggles the snow would have stung his eyes in seconds and he would have been forced to retreat and look through the smudged side window of the cab. This way his visibility was at least twice the distance.

He decided to keep the speed down to about 40 miles per hour and so far the journey had been uneventful. The signals had all been in their favour and so had all of the crossings. They had travelled uneventfully out of London and through the Midlands; they were now well up country on their way to York. The time was past midnight.

George was the first to speak. He called to Percy who was at the back of the tender, scuffting the coal forward with an elephant's tab shovel.

"I think the weather's taken a real turn for the worse," he shouted.

Percy grunted, made his way to the cab and looked out into the thick curtain of snow that was the night. George shouted above the wind: "We'll stop at the signal box just past Shepherd's bend, two miles before York. We'll get him to phone and tell York Station to set the points ready for us coming in for the night," shouted George.

Percy grunted mater-of-factly: "Should have done it at Watford junction four hours ago," and carried on scuffting the coal forward ready to throw into the firebox.

"We'll drop the speed down to 25 mph and take it even slower for the last few miles," said George.

Percy looked out again and shivered. "It must be between six and nine inches deep on the fields by now," he said. "It's snowing like 'ell and the wind's enough to cut a man in two! I wouldn't like to be out working in it tonight," he added with a chuckle.

The cab was as warm as toast, the huge lumps of shiny, Welsh steam coal burned brightly in the firebox keeping the whole area aglow. George pointed Percy towards the area above the funnel where the red-hot embers were reflected in the falling snowflakes. George shouted to Percy that the sky had turned pink. An eerie pink glow seemed to surround the whole locomotive giving it a surreal feel. It was just one of those wonderful moments they lived for whilst driving a train.

The distance to York was about six miles now. It was virtually flat for four miles followed by a one mile gentle decline at 1:60. The decline finally steepening down through a pretty valley with a tight curve at the bottom called Shepherd's Bend.

Their speed on the flat was now approaching 43 mph so George touched the brakes very gently to start bringing the giant's speed down to the planned 25mph. There was little or no drive required from the engine on the flat for the locomotive of 120 tons had a momentum of its own and was running effortlessly, just being topped up by the steam power.

George was surprised when he touched the lever; there seemed to be no response from the brakes. Not that feeling of complete control over this powerful stallion he was so used to. Uneasiness gripped his stomach. Not understanding, George touched the brakes again. Sensitivity was the name of the game, for a skid could be disastrous even on the flat. The brake lever responded by becoming very loose in George's hand. He jumped off the little seat and faced the controls full on. Now adrenaline was pumping instantaneously through his whole body.

Frantically, he pushed the lever forward… nothing. Then he pulled the lever back… nothing. The brake lever wasn't connected to anything.

The speed was now approaching 46 mph. 46 mph wasn't a problem on the flat but the incline was approaching. George had to slow the locomotive before it tipped its nose down the incline followed by seven carriages with 40 something passengers on its way down to Shepherd's Bend. Once on the incline, he would have lost control altogether and the only brakes would be prayers.

George screamed over the wind to Percy, "Perc, we've lost our brakes!"

Like a flash Percy was alongside him watching George fruitlessly push and pull the impotent lever backwards and forwards.

Percy tried with the same result. An unspoken anxiety was eating away at both of them.

"Handbrake?"

George spun the hand brake wheel around and around. Nothing!

"How far to the incline?"

"'bout two miles now."

"F***"

Percy shouted: "We've got 43 passengers fast asleep and at the bottom of the incline we'll be hitting Shepherd's Bend at close on 70mph. Even if we do stay on the tracks, which will be a bloody miracle, there'll be half the passengers tumbling out of their bunk beds onto the floor. There'll be more broken bones than at an A & E department in Glasgow on Burns' Night!"

George ignored what he was saying, his mind was racing. There was always the steam control. George released the valve and spun it wildly, the steam gushed out of the system enveloping the engine. The 120 tons of moving locomotive and carriages now had to drive the heavy steam engine through the wheels by its own momentum. This would act as a huge brake on the whole train. There was an immediate reduction in the speed. 46mph reduced down to 44mph. George could feel cold beads of sweat running down his back.

Now they had to wait and see if the drag on the engine was sufficient to stop the train before the incline. The weather was becoming worse and worse as the snow blew into the small cab. Travelling at any speed above 40 miles an hour made the snow race past the cab but as the train slowed the snow began to enter. Visibility forward was down to only a few yards in front of the engine even with goggles; the rails were completely covered by snow. If it wasn't for the telegraph poles and hedges, George would have been at a loss as to where the train was going next.

44mph dropped down to 38mph, still much too fast.

George and Percy were quiet in their own worlds when George suggested Percy make his way back through the tender and the train to the cabin of the railway Company Engineer and warn him of the impending crash. At first Percy thought the idea was a stupid one but then it dawned on him. The engineer may have another solution to the situation so he hurried through the coal tender's narrow corridor and was soon out of sight.

George was left alone watching the speedometer needle drop again; 36mph, 35mph, 34mph. Cutting off the steam had been the right thing to do. It was the only thing to do. It was working. Knowing there was no patron saint of railway workers, George offered a prayer up to the Almighty. In his head, he went over and over the checks he had made at King's Cross Station before they set off. He was absolutely positive everything had been working. Thinking back though, there had been no need to apply the brakes so far for the whole journey; the signals had been with them and the also the crossings. The brakes could have become defective any time in the last four hours.

Percy collected a sleepy Albert Jennings on his way through the carriages and together they quickly made their way to Carston's cabin. Percy didn't stand on ceremony and with Albert they banged loudly on Dr Prestwick's door. Carston nearly fell out of their narrow bed with the noise. Celia covered herself up as he went out into the corridor fastening his dressing gown as he went. The whole, 'lost brakes, imminent incline, Shepherd's Bend' story tumbled out of Percy's mouth in whistled, incomprehensible Glaswegian. Carston looked at Albert. Albert interpreted.

Carston thought for a moment and then said: "Get everyone out of their cabins and into the last two carriages. They'll be the carriages that will take the least impact when we crash. Make sure everyone takes a pillow and wrap it around his or her neck to protect their heads. Get them to huddle together so they can't tumble around in the carriage when it goes over."

Carston went deep in thought then, because neither of them had moved, he shouted: "DO IT NOW!"

Albert and Percy raced off down the corridor banging on every cabin door, not waiting for a reply but opening them and shouting instructions to the sleeping passengers.

Back into his own carriage, Carston grabbed his trousers and put on his gabardine raincoat telling Celia to put on as many clothes as she could as quickly as she could and make her way to the last carriage: "And don't forget to take your pillow and wrap it tightly around your neck". Then he kissed her passionately, told her he loved her and ran off towards the front of the train.

She was about to protest but thought better of it. This was Carston's world and here was a situation she could not possibly understand. The urgency in his voice demanded action and action right now! Not protests. As she dressed, Celia ran over some of the conversation she had sleepily overheard between Albert and Carston. There was something about, 'no brakes, a bend and too fast'. Here were enough danger words to urge her to dress at top speed. Once dressed and in her topcoat she made her way towards the back of the train helping the young and the elderly back to the last two carriages. Those passengers who protested she ignored and moved on to the next carriage to help them.

Soon there was a steady stream of passengers making their way to the rear of the train. Even the protesters started to join the orderly snake of people all carrying their pillows.

Carston appeared from the narrow coal tender tunnel into the cab of the locomotive. George didn't know how Carston's rude awakening had been received so stood aside to let the engineer see the controls.

The greetings were short: "Carston."

George replied: "George, sir."

They engaged in a cursory handshake.

The speed had dropped to 22mph and fortunately was dropping quickly: "How far to the incline?" shouted Carston above the wind.

"'bout 800 yards sir."

"Will it be far enough?"

"Not sure, sir."

20mph, 18mph, 17mph.

Both men watched helplessly as the dial dropped. Carston leaned out of the cab into the snowstorm but couldn't see a thing.

George passed him his goggles: "These'll help sir." Before he leaned out a second time he tapped the speedometer dial. It had dropped to 15mph.

Carston leaned out and saw the 300-yard distance marker to the top of the incline slowly pass them by.

12mph, 11mph, 10mph.

The locomotive seemed slow enough to walk alongside, the huge train lumbering slower and slower.

"I think we're going to be OK, sir," ventured George. Then they both watched the 100-yard distance marker pass by even more slowly.

But all too quickly the actual incline marker was upon them with its lazy arm painted white with the black numbers 1:60 pointed ominously down the incline.

The locomotive edged to the top of the incline stopping on the cusp...only to be edged gently over by the momentum of the following, gently bumping carriages. First, the engine front four bogey wheels rolled onto the incline, followed by the main locomotive. Eight huge wheels followed on to the incline. The coal tender front wheels followed then the coal tender back wheels.

George and Carston looked at each other as the train eased itself onto the incline. The whole event was happening in slow motion. There was absolutely nothing they could do.

The mph dial that had so slowly dropped to zero was now frighteningly making its way back up the dial.

3mph, 5mph, 7mph.

A sweating Percy joined them on the footplate. And shouted: "Nearly all the passengers are in the last two carriages all wrapped up in pillows. There's an awful lot of crying and screaming going on from some but they are about as safe as they could ever be for what's coming. We were so, so close to stopping. What pushed us over?"

"The bumping of the carriages."

"What happens now?" shouted George to Carston

"We pray."

12mph 15mph 21mph

Carston calculated that the whole train was probably now on the gradient and the speed would rise exponentially.

Back in the last two carriages the passengers were huddled together on the seats, on the floor and in the narrow corridors. Each passenger had travelled the full sinusoidal wave of emotions; anxiety that the train wouldn't stop in time, elation that it had stopped and a cheer that the awful possibility of a crash had been averted. Then the dreadful realisation that the train had edged over the brow and was heading down the incline gathering speed.

A silence settled as they listened to the noise of the train building up speed down the incline.

Clickety-click, clickety-click, clickety-click, clickety-click, clickety-click

The crying had stopped; the screaming had stopped, all that could be heard were muffled prayers coming from the elderly. Celia held a little girl tightly in her lap humming to her. The little girl's mother held onto her other two children all with pillows wrapped around their necks looking to Celia for reassurance. Celia smiled weakly. Frightened, big brown innocent eyes looked up at Celia trying to understand.

Back in the cab the three men watched the dial 24mph, 28mph, 32mph.

They were about half way down the incline heading for Shepherd's Bend when the locomotive came out of the cutting and the protection of the trees. The train was met by a howl of wind and snow, there being no protection whatsoever. It had been snowing hard all day in the valley and the wind had collected the snow from all the surrounding fields and packed it solidly up to a height of about 20ft against the railway cutting side forming a huge snowdrift across the track.

It was Carston who was looking out at the moment of impact and was thrown hard against the front of the cab. As the train ploughed into the packed snow it sliced two shavings off the snowdrift that curled into both sides of the open locomotive cab. The cab filled with snow in an instant. The train surged on through the 40yds of solid snow drift; a huge powerhouse of steel momentum pushing against Mother Nature's white wall. The train carved its way onwards with the snow packing into the tiny cab until the men could hardly breathe.

But the snow was winning, for the first time that night the snow was on their side. The powerhouse of steel was slowing down. All its out-of-control-energy from the incline gradually became expended as it freewheeled on into the unforgiving snow. Suddenly, out the other end of the huge snowdrift the locomotive engine emerged.

5mph, 3mph, 1mph eventually shuddering to a stop.

Percy had dived into the tender corridor when the snow started to curl menacingly into the cab. Even in there he was waist deep in packed snow in the tiny corridor. When the locomotive finally came to a stop he found he couldn't go forwards to the cab so he kicked open the corridor back door. He climbed nimbly as a cat up the iron-rung ladder on the back of the coal tender and jumped onto the mountain of coal. Sliding forward down the heap he grabbed his spare shovel on the way down. Once in the snow filled cab he started to dig the snow away from where he had last seen George. Two minutes of hard digging, by a man who shovelled for a living, paid off and George was soon free. Percy then turned his attentions to Carston who was unconscious and bleeding from the blow to his head when the locomotive first hit the snowdrift. Percy completely cleared the locomotive cab of snow and made both men as comfortable as possible.

And then everything fell strangely silent. The wind suddenly dropped and only a few flurries of snow settled on the exhausted trio. The situation was surreal. Peacefulness as though the last few minutes had never happened. A bad dream left behind in the night. It had all happened to someone else. Somewhere else, over there and they somehow had been onlookers. The three men sat in their uncomfortable positions on the cramped cab floor and just looked at each other with the realisation of, what might have been.

Back in the last two carriages the impact of the crash into the snow had been minimised because the passengers were packed so tightly into the compartments. The pillows had been a Godsend. Celia was one of the first to move to see if the engine had been crushed in the impact but could see nothing; they were in a complete tunnel of snow. Whichever window she looked out of all she could see was packed snow. Passengers began getting up and helping each other to their feet.

The comments that always follow successful outcomes of potentially very serious situations began to be uttered: 'Well it wasn't all that bad.' 'Could have stayed in our cabins at a push.' 'Lot of fuss about nothing in the end, if you ask me.' Celia ignored them all. They could say what they like... now.

Celia reverted to high alert as she started to feel a sudden drop in temperature. All the passengers started to feel the biting cold at the same time. The temperature was plummeting because all the pipes that carried the heating system had been torn from between the coaches by the snow. At first, because everyone was packed in so tightly the temperature drop wasn't so apparent, but as they started to move away from each other, the cold air found its way into the gaps between the passengers and through the clothes of the hurriedly dressed. Celia was the first to understand what was happening and quickly closed all of the internal doors. Passengers were beginning to shiver for all of the carriages were still in the snowdrift. They were in a tunnel of snow.

Only the engine was through to the other side. It was as if all the carriages were in a tubular refrigerator. Celia wrapped the children up as tightly as she could and ran to the nearest cabin ripping the blankets off the beds and racing back to the last two carriages and distributing them to the young and the elderly.
She realised she couldn't do it all on her own so enlisted help from Albert and some of the younger men. She knew all she was doing was containing the situation. But it would get worse if she didn't do something.

Once she was happy that the elderly passengers and children were getting the blankets, she took it upon herself to run all of the way to the front of the train to see if there was anything she could do. Having never needed to get through to the engine of a train before, she had no idea what to do. She opened the last, front carriage door and was faced by the back of the coal tender. She shouted and shouted. Just as she was about to climb the set of iron loops that passed for steps Percy poked his head out of the tender passage way. He helped her through the cramped passage to the cab.

Carston was just coming to. Celia dropped to her knees and cradled his head. She sobbed at the sight of so much blood and gently moved his blood-soaked hair out of his eyes. Carston was in that land between consciousness and unconsciousness. A strange land where pain is intermittent, but as the body moves slowly back towards consciousness and continuous hurt it desperately tries to return to its more peaceful pain-free, unconscious state. Then it recognises familiar faces and noises and reluctantly agrees to re-join the land of the awake.

Percy spoke first: "He's OK miss. All head wounds bleed a lot."

She examined the cut, which by now had stopped bleeding, and covered the wound with a pad made of his handkerchief. He smiled limply at her and she hugged him to take away the hurt as a mother does with a small child.

Remembering the rest of the passengers, Celia asked if there was a way they could get some heat into the carriages. Percy looked at the fire: "There should be some heat getting through unless the pipes have been ripped off."

"Everybody is safe and well after the crash but they're freezing back there," explained Celia.

It was then that George spoke: "We need to get out of here. Them folks are packed in snow like cod in ice on a trawler. If we don't get them out soon the result will be far worse than the crash ever would have been. They'll all be froze to death!"

"How with no brakes?" asked Percy.

"We're virtually at the bottom of the incline now. There's no chance of her running away so let's get up steam and just limp the last two miles to York. It's flat all the way and if we phone from the signal box they can send another engine to be our brakes."

"How long to get up steam?" whispered Carston now fully conscious.

"10 minutes if we get our skates on," said Percy. And with that he reached for his shovel flicked open the fire door, regulated the draught in the firebox to maximum and started to cast the coal inside.

A gentle roar started as the cold night wind fanned the flames.

After a few minutes of continuous shovelling with sweat dripping from his face Percy declared: "There, in a few moments we can be on our way." There was nothing else they could do so George instructed Percy to go to the back of the train and tell everybody what was happening.

Celia, Carston and George watched the mercury indicating the steam pressure rise steadily in the glass.

When it was as high as it needed to be George released the flow of dry sand onto the rails in front of each wheel for such occasions and pushed the drive lever slowly forward...

Nothing.

He eased the drive lever back and engaged reverse. When reverse was fully engaged, he eased the drive lever forward again. The loco backed up about 6ft bumping the carriages together, taking up all of the slack back into the snowdrift. Into forward again and this time George pushed the drive lever as far forward as it would go. The carriages bumped forwards in turn taking up the slack. The snow tunnel suddenly collapsed releasing its grip on the carriages.

With wheels spinning, the locomotive jolted forward dragging its snow-covered load. The speed picked up to 3 mph and the ice-cold train, with the carriages still piled high with snow, crept forward out of its icy tomb on its way around Shepherd's Bend and slowly to the signal box. The signalman was amazed to see the strange sight coming out of the darkness. He frantically rang York alerting them of the situation.

20 minutes later, the night locomotive service to Scotland pulled into York Station to be met by a mass of emergency services waiting on the platform.

8 Examination of the Locomotive

Carston, with bandaged head and against all doctor's orders, ducked under the police tape to get nearer to the previous night's locomotive. His head was stinging from 12 stitches in his forehead and a night in hospital rather than with his wife, because he had been concussed.

A rotund railway policeman approached him but allowed him through when shown Carston's ID. To Carston's amazement both George and Percy were already there doing exactly what he was going to do.

"Morning. Busy old night wasn't it? Found anything?"

"Nothing really," said Percy sarcastically, "only both sets of brakes sawn through. Whoever did it had no regard for the number of people they were likely to kill. The bastards."

"Oxyacetylene cut through or hacksaw cut through?" demanded Carston.

"Hacksaw."

"Then whoever did it must have been at it for some time."

Carston was led to the offending steelwork and came to the same conclusion as George and Percy.

The steelwork had been cut virtually through and just left 1/16 of an inch for the cursory check whilst stationary. As soon as the brakes were applied for real they would have snapped like Barry Island rock.

George was shaking his head slowly when Carston broke his train of thought,

"Penny for them?"

George looked up slowly and said: "As I've grown older it's become harder and harder to frighten me. But this frightened me. Someone out there is prepared to kill or maim about 40 innocent people to achieve something. What is there in this world that can possibly have that level of value?" Whatever did they want to achieve? Who could do such a thing? Has life become that cheap?" George wasn't speaking to anyone in particular; rather he was speaking to mankind and reflecting on how low it had sunk.

Carston tried to break his melancholy mood: "Whatever the reason, there are 40-odd people who are alive today as a result of your quick thinking. The likelihood is that a less cautious driver would have waited to brake the train until they were much closer to the incline. We wouldn't have stood a chance at the bend and the outcome is too horrible to imagine." George was mulling the comment over when a policeman came over and asked if Dr Prestwick would follow him to the York Station Master's office. Carston smiled his gratitude to George patting him on his arm as he passed.

In the office were three men. Sitting behind the Station Master's desk, in the Station Master's own chair, (much to his chagrin) sat a pinstriped suited, government official. The suited man said: "If you would all beso kind as to leave except Dr Prestwick, I would be very grateful."

To have someone sitting in his chair was bad enough for the Station Master.To be told to get out of his own office was more than body and soul could bear and he huffed and puffed his resentment as he left.

When alone, the suited man gestured for Carston to sit down. He explained he worked for MI5. There were some unsubstantiated reports that Prestwick's work had reached the ears of some unpleasant foreign powers. For his own safety he would have to return to London forthwith.

"Do you think my work and the locomotive incident are connected?"

"Who knows, but whoever did it must have thought there was something on board of great value, or someone on board who was one of their targets. Were you carrying any secret documents or plans or the like?"

"I'll bet you took the MI5 manual on your honeymoon," snapped an irritated Carston. "Are you saying I could be the target?" he asked incredulously.

"Who knows at this stage? We'll do some further checking and info gathering and see what that uncovers."

Carston argued with the suited man to no avail. His honeymoon was not a matter of national consideration. He was going back to London one way or another. Carston repeated all of his arguments but the suited man was not budging.

"How long have I got?" asked Carston resignedly.

"Your train leaves for London in two hours. Be on it!"

Carston was about to leave the office when the suited man called him back.

"By the way, you will be working from now on under a Dr Hollingsworth, another steam expert,who will meet you at King's Cross Station."

The announcement to Celia in the Railway Hotel bedroom went exactly as he had dreaded. She cried when he told her. She shouted it wasn't fair; no bride would understand. She tried to persuade him to stay but eventually she knew he had no choice.

What he did suggest was she continue on to Fort William to see her parents who she hadn't seen for two years and then re-join him in London in two weeks.

They stayed very close together for the little time they had left until he couldn't leave it another moment longer to catch the train.

9
A Lonely Hotel Meal

Celia idly twisted her hair as she sat alone picking at her lukewarm dinner in the empty hotel restaurant. Tonight the railway hotel, despite its turn-of-the-century splendour, was the loneliest place on God's earth. The branded EPNS cutlery was dull tonight. The crystal glasses didn't shine tonight and the heavy brocade drapes were not fashionable wall coverings, tonight they hung like shrouds. Such was Celia's understandable mood. Such would have been the mood of any solitary, day-old bride.

This was not what she had envisaged on her honeymoon, but she also knew it wasn't what Carston wanted either. The tears of resignation eventually dried and she started to plan her onward journey. Thumbing through the train timetable alongside her, logo embossed dinner plate, she discovered the next train to Scotland was leaving at 06.30 am the following day and then the next train was a two-day delay because of the weekend. That was enough of a prompt for her, so she finished her unappetising meal quickly, called at the reception desk to settle the bill and retired for an early start the next day. There was nothing to pay as the train company had settled the bill on behalf of all of the passengers who were on that fateful overnight train journey.

Not to be delayed the following morning Celia requested the receptionist return the pendant and music box and other valuables she had deposited. She collected the presents and made her way to her room.

In her, expansive, high ceilinged hotel bedroom, she slumped down into a big leather armchair and with her carefully manicured fingers gently wound up Carston's music box and lifted the lid. She fingered the ornate marquetry on the beautiful music box lid. It was perched on the wide arm of the chair and she imagined Carston smiling at her from the other enormous armchair as it played his favourite tune. Somehow she didn't feel so lonely. She opened the little drawer that housed the other barrels and absently touched the small spigots that pinged the tuning fork-like notes. There were four barrels, Edelweiss, which was currently playing, Cantata 208, Moonlight Sonata, and another barrel that had no label.

She played each in turn and smiled to herself. When she came to play the last tune it didn't sound like anything she could recall. It just seemed like a random set of notes so she wondered if she was playing it too slowly or had put the barrel in the wrong way round. But tiredness by this time was beginning to catch up with her so she packed everything she could away in her case ready for an early start. When she opened the wardrobe to pack her clothes she noted that they were all at the end of the wardrobe rail that Carston's clothes had previously hung upon. Strange, she thought to herself, he must have moved them all over when he packed in such a rush. She smiled to herself at the reason for the rush.

She smiled at the memory of her lying naked and beckoning to him from under the covers of the bed, in the middle of the afternoon. She smiled at the memory of him purposefully striding towards the bedroom door on his way to catch the train, case in one hand, coat draped over his other arm, stopping, being seduced back for just one more kiss which led to another kiss and another, then having to get dressed again even more quickly, collecting his luggage again and running for the door. She had even tried tears to coax him to miss his train. It had been a wonderful afternoon, just the two of them. But, oh, so short.

Eventually, Celia fell fast asleep but was rudely woken by the hotel telephone jangling with her early alarm call. Breakfast was outside her room and soon she found herself sitting on the train heading to see her parents. She had mixed feelings. On one hand she so dearly wanted to see her mother and father after such a long time but already she missed Carston. She so wanted to introduce him to her father. She was proud of both her parents but felt Carston and her father would have had so many things in common to talk about.

Her parents were thrilled to see her and fired questions at her one after another. When her mother stopped to draw breath her father fired question after question. There was so much catching up to do. Three days into her stay with her parents they decided to visit her favourite uncle. This uncle she really liked. He was full of fun and had teased her all through her childhood. Being a carpenter by trade his house was full of amazing things he'd made like children's toys, games, furniture and carvings. Just as the three of them were leaving to catch the bus Celia rushed back into the house to take Carston's music box for her uncle to see the exquisite marquetry. She knew he'd love it.

Her uncle now lived on his own but made scones and tea for them. Throughout the meal she answered all the same questions again about what she had been doing in London. He listened avidly to all her stories of university life and London life. Life was so different in Fort William. The grass grew, the paint peeled, the rain fell and the numbers in the little kirk dwindled.

Eventually, it was time to leave and he hugged her and told her he had missed her and would she come again next time and this time be sure to bring her young man with her. He passed the music box back to her, said it was a beautiful piece of work and if anyone had bought it for him he would know that person loved him dearly.

As soon as they returned to her parents' house they could see something was wrong. The back door of the house was ajar. Celia's father went in first and came out ashen. They had been burgled. Celia's mother rushed next door to phone the police. On investigation the police decided the burglar had been interrupted, for he had only gone into Celia's room. As far as they could see nothing had been taken.

To be burgled was unheard of in their little sleepy village outside Fort William so a feeling of unease was creeping over her.

The incident left her two parents shaken and they decided to change all the locks in the house and put bolts on all the doors. Celia's carpenter uncle was back at the house the very next day when he heard, fitting all the new security for them. Celia tried to explain that lightening never struck twice but her logic fell on very unsettled ears.

10
The Platform Meeting

Carston's train arrived in King's Cross Station, on time, to the minute, unlike his previous journey. He mused over how grown-up Celia had eventually been when he had to cut their honeymoon so short. They had spent some time together but nothing would have taken the place of the holiday she had planned for them. She was to show him off to everyone in her village and her relatives for the first week then just the two of them head for a ski resort and ski till they dropped. He did feel sorry for her and the last memory of her was with tears in her eyes waving him off from the bed.

He struggled to retrieve his case from the luggage rack but was soon swinging open the carriage door onto the platform. There seemed to be hundreds of people on the platform all either getting off or meeting someone. How was he to recognise this Dr Hollingsworth in all these crowds?

Carston was in the wrong place; he should be with his bride. His patience was strained and he was in no mood to meet some academic after a long, long train journey.

The idea of working with someone else did nothing to inspire him. Carston wasn't used to working with anyone at all. He worked alone. If he wanted to work all night then, he would. If his research wasn't going right and he needed a break, he took one. Working under a prof he didn't know and, for that matter, had never even heard of, did his spirits no good at all. He needed a drink and if this prof didn't show up fairly soon then he was going to head for a bar in the station and wait there.

As he ordered his second scotch a voice behind he made him turn: "Dr Carston Prestwick?"

"Yes?"

"I'm Professor Jill Hollingsworth and I'll have whatever you're having."

Standing behind him was a woman in her late twenties with long, dark, tied back shiny hair. Her skin was that lovely Mediterranean olive colour that women crave for and men desire. She smiled as she reached out to shake his hand. With coins in one hand and his drink in the other he fumbled about trying to put one down. It was Prof Hollingsworth who took the drink from his hand allowing him to shake hers. After getting another drink they made their way to his table and sat opposite each other.

"Well, you're not exactly what I was expecting."

"And what was that, pray? A whiskery old gent wearing a monocle dressed in a long, old coat carrying a gamp?"

Carston was out of order and knew it: "No, I don't know any professors of steam locomotion who are women that's all."

"Does it bother you?"

"No, why should it?"

"You're the flustered one." There was a long pause.

"Please may we start again?" asked Carston.

"I'm Jill Hollingsworth."

"And I'm Carston Prestwick and I'm very pleased to meet you."

"Now I feel better."

"Me too. You eaten?"

"Not really, only snacks on the train."

"Good, let's go and find a restaurant, I'm starving," she said.

Carston followed her out of the station bar. Her camel coat was not the coat of an academic, her shape was not the shape of an academic and her Mediterranean looks were not the looks of an academic. Well, not the academics he had been used to anyway. They were more the whiskery, monocle types carrying a gamp. And those were the women, he smiled to himself.

The days flew by with Carston and Jill working on different projects on the same locomotive. Carston was surprised by her knowledge of railways and her colourful upbringing by her father. She had worked on the most amazing railways in the world. Her experience put his experience into the shadows. She was a real grafter of an engineer and Carston admired this in her. Occasionally, when he was ready to stop she wanted to stay to complete things. They worked early in the mornings and worked late at night. Regularly they both went out on the trials through the night when special expertise was required.

But in the evenings when he was back in his dreary flat, Carston missed Celia terribly and to start with telephoned her regularly. However, both he and Celia believed the bored Scottish telephone exchange operator was eavesdropping on their crackly phone conversations so both were reluctant to say what they really meant. Pockets full of pennies were fed into the black, telephone box and the pips seemed to go off every few seconds. Carston's thumb was numb at the end of each call from incessantly pressing the button marked A to add money and continue the call. Their inadequate calls became less frequent as they were both too embarrassed to say what they wanted to say to each other and his hours of work became protracted. They settled on one stilted call every three days.

But one good thing happened during this fraught time. Percy and George were each awarded bravery medals for their action on that fateful night. Following the annual general meeting of The Ancient and Venerable Association of Railwaymen under the heading of Any Other Business, the two of them were invited to come to the podium to receive their medals.

Despite his protestations George was dressed in a new suit. His wife believed he would have preferred to go up for the presentation in a boiler suit and his old leather cap, but this was a proud moment for them and the occasion demanded   a new suit for him and definitely a new outfit for her. George was called forward first and despite his obvious discomfort, a huge round of applause followed him to the front. When the citation was read aloud he stood, head bowed listening to the seriousness of the situation, reliving every moment. Percy was next and stood to attention at the podium, eyes looking forward, sporting a chest full of medals from his time during the First World War. After they had been awarded their medals the whole audience rose to their feet as one and gave the pair a standing ovation. Lots of shuffling from the shy George and Percy stood to attention throughout reflecting their different backgrounds. Tears of pride flowed down George's wife's face.

A drinks reception followed the ceremony accompanied by lots of backslapping. George couldn't wait to leave but Percy settled in for the duration. Not often was Percy honoured to a free drinks reception and he was going to enjoy every moment.

Carston and the whole Rosser's Board had their photographs taken with the pair for posterity and a cheque for £100 was awarded to each. In George's wife's mind's eye she saw a new three-piece suite for their front room and Percy saw bar bills being settled at every pub in his neighbourhood.

It was a good day.

***

Ten days passed in the South Ruislip depot with Carston and Jill working at 100% when a crisis occurred. An internal security breach had been discovered and classified documents stolen. It left Carston and Jill so unnerved they worked late into the night locking up important information, checking what had been stolen and destroying copies of everything. When eventually they finished the tedious task, they agreed they both needed to get something to eat, then Jill could get a taxi home. The last thing either of them wanted when they got home was to set about cooking.

As they went out into the London night Jill discovered the phenomena called, London smog. Not to be defeated, they felt their way to a small café and ordered, hoping the smog would be clearer when their meal was finished. Wine prolonged the meal and for the first time since they started working together they really relaxed in each other's company. Her childhood on the great railways of Europe was recounted in detail and Carston listened in awe. In turn he told her of his exploits at university and suddenly the second bottle was dry.

Wrapped up and stepping out again into the London smog, which had thickened impossibly, they began the fruitless task of trying to find a taxi for her. Carston waved down the only taxi they saw that was travelling at less than two miles an hour in the soupy weather. The angry taxi driver remonstrated that Carston must want to get killed jumping out like that. He wouldn't take any more fares, he already had two fares squashed in his cab and that was only because they were both on his way home. He drove off, his foul temper compounded by the weather.

Carston's flat was within walking distance of the cafe, there was no decision to make, there was no alternative; the weather was just too bad. Jill was to stay at his flat till the morning.

She took his arm and together they laughed at the silliness of it all. Expending all their efforts to get a steam engine to travel at higher and higher speeds and Mother Nature could bring everything down to a 'feeling your way forward pace'. They fumbled and stumbled along the murky roads where white streetlights way above their heads were of no value whatsoever.

After several wrong turns in the completely disorienting night they found his front door. Keys clinked in the locks and suddenly they were inside the warm, welcome flat. Carston took her coat and poured them both a large whisky to accompany them on the visitor's tour. They joked about tossing a coin for the sofa which looked about as appealing as the pavement. Jill was inwardly comparing Carston's spacious flat with her own studio and felt his flat had the edge, and a kitchen too!

As he was coming out of the tiny dining room and she was passing him to have a look inside, they had to squeeze past each other in the narrow doorway. Facing each other, in that warm closeness, the world around them stopped for a second; the cold weather, the problems of work, the unnerving smog, everything stopped. Each carrying a freshly poured large whisky and having consumed two bottles of wine with the meal between them, there was no world outside. The only world was here, and the only world was now. Without taking their eyes off each other they chinked glasses in the tight doorway.

11

Major Brown and Pickering Alone

in the Board Room

Westerman's head of security, Pickering never wrote reports and was careful that none of his conversations were ever recorded. In the time he had been working for this chairman he had been involved in a number, of what could, at best be considered dubious and at worst, downright dishonest operations. He had quickly learned there must never be any audit trail back to the Chairman or, more importantly, him. Now in the boardroom with just the Chairman he reported.

"It's true sir, Prestwick's dissertation had been withdrawn from the university shelves just as Shawcross said, apparently, about 10 weeks ago."

Major Brown snorted: "10 bloody weeks ago. There's no chance of finding it now is there?"

"No sir. We could probably put our hands on the odd chapter that might be lying about in his flat but it's unlikely to reveal much on its own."

"What about the South Ruislip Depot?"

"Well sir, we did the third reconnoitre of the site last night. It's so well guarded it makes the crown jewels look as though they are about as safe as if they were in an allotment shed!"

"What the Hell can be so secret?" asked Major Brown, absently lighting another cigar even though there was one still burning in the huge ashtray.
Then he remembered something and said absently: "Oh, there is one way we can find out what they are doing in there but I'll only use it as a last resort."

"There are dogs all around the site," Pickering continued, "nobody goes in or out except one steam engine. A steam engine that has no name and no serial number."

"We need to get a look inside that engine, and if we can't get inside the depot then we'll wait till it comes out," said Major Brown determinedly.

"Set up a railway crossing accident or something. Something that would slow the engine down to a stop and make the guards leave their posts to sort it out.

Then, while they're off, we send our people in, reverse the engine way back down the track so that Shawcross can take a good hard look at it."

"Whatever you say sir. But these guys who are going to steal the engine mustn't be associated with us in any way. It'll cost big time."

"Do it. Just bloody well do it, whatever it costs!"

12 Back in the Antique Shop

The ancient servant's bell attached to the frame of the dingy, London antique shop front door announced the return of Hans and the weasel man.

"Well? Have you got it?" came the snapped demand from the far end of the shop before the bell had stopped ringing.

"Well, err, no," replied Hans feeling like a schoolboy in front of his headmaster.

"No? No? Why not? How difficult can it possibly be to steal a music box from a woman?"

The short, bald, elderly man behind the desk at the far end of the shop stood up abruptly knocking over his chair, distressed beyond reason by the news. His

Napoleon syndrome and vicious tongue had stood him in good stead as he had scrabbled up through the ranks throughout his miserable, lonely career. But now all his rank and seniority was slipping away because of a stupid mistake made on his watch.

Reports of the loss of the music box would have rocketed up through the ranks of his country's secret service as bad news always did and retribution on him would be returning equally fast down the ranks. Normally, he would have expected an immediate recall to the Motherland. He had only two saving graces. One stood before him in the form of two undercover officers who instilled no confidence in him whatsoever. His only other saving grace was his well-established cover in the form of the antique shop and the fact that the operation was too far advanced to replace him...he hoped. He desperately needed the music box to be back in his hands as soon as possible to redeem himself.

A well-rehearsed reply followed from Hans: "Amazingly, in the whole of London we were able work out who the woman was who bought the music box from here. We calculated what her movements were going to be because, after intensive investigation by us, we found out she was getting married and travelling to Scotland for her honeymoon with her new husband on the night train from London."

"Well, first we had the train doctored in London by some people we know and waited in the most ferocious snowy weather for the train to derail at a sharp bend near York where, in the confusion of the crash, we were going to get into the carriages and retrieve the music box. God only knows how, but by some miracle, it didn't crash. Because of the foul weather the train was grounded in York and all the passengers put up in hotels. The woman's new husband was sent back to London on another train the following day for some reason, so we searched her room while she was at dinner... Nothing! The music box must have been in the hotel safe or he must have taken it back to London with him. We caught the same train as her the following day and travelled all the way to Fort William waiting for another opportunity. It came. We searched through her things while she and her parents were out... Nothing!"

The little man was becoming more and more agitated, his face twitching in temper at the list of excuses.

Then Hans continued: "We concluded that her husband must have taken it with him back to London. We'll search his flat on Saturday and get it then. It will be back with you by Monday, we're confident."

There was a long pause, which the visitors interpreted as a reprieve, their shoulders slackening perceptibly, but it was actually the man behind the desk holding back convulsions. He was beside himself, his temper boiling in a cocktail of angst for his future and rage.

"You have failed me!" exploded the parchment faced, wizened old man struggling to find the words in a second language, "but much worse you have failed your Mother country. The retrieval of the music box is of immense national importance. You must not fail again! Whatever the cost it must be found. Failure for you will mean immediate repatriation and being moved to the front line."

They all knew this was a death sentence by another name.

The old man continued, saliva dribbling down one side of his mouth as he tried to control himself: "The man they call Hawk will be coming here in three days to plan the next stage of the operation which will set the British Government back three years in their war effort, by which time we will be dominant. You must not fail to have it in my hands ready for him by Monday."

Once again the two men left the antique shop into the drizzle of an even blacker London night.

13 The Signal Box

The sleepy white signal box with its flaking paint and rickety steps hid the fact that inside it was warm as toast. On the top of the glowing stove a chipped, red, enamelled kettle started to puff out anaemic steam. The big signalman struggled out of his comfortable, worn chair complete with threadbare arms and lumbered over to a half open cupboard. There he spooned a heaped spoonful of Yorkshire tea into a grubby, earthenware, brown teapot and then another, 'for the pot'. He reached for the wooden biscuit barrel from the shelf and placed two ginger nuts on the peeling Formica table by the side of his armchair and proceeded to drop three heaped spoonsful of sugar into his huge, brown, tea-stained mug. Hesitating momentarily on the third spoonful of sugar he put a few grains of Tate and Lyle back into the blue and white packet, a gesture to his ever-increasing waistband and a sop to his ever-complaining wife.

He knew exactly what she would have said had she seen the state of his tea-making utensils. Piece by piece they would have taken flight out of the nearest window, mug, teapot and kettle. A pristine, matching set of tea-making equipment would have replaced it the very next day but the tea wouldn't have tasted nearly as good! Mashing tackle needs years of breaking in, something she would never have understood. He smiled to himself over her concern for him and decided to call in and get a bar of her favourite chocolate on his way home. She did look after him he thought and he loved her dearly for all her concerns.

The red kettle seemed to be taking forever so he left the hob saying to nobody in particular, 'a watch pot...' Opening the signal box back door he walked out onto the narrow wooden veranda to savour the night and its familiar sounds. The stars were bright between the clouds and the moon lay on its back so he turned the change over in his pocket just as his mother had taught him, 'for good fortune'. Working nights regularly he recognised the individual calls of the owls and waited for the far off replies. He could smell rain in the air. He shuddered in the cold night air and was about to abandon his sojourn and return to his cosy signal box when he heard the sound of a far off lorry engine.

What made him stop and listen longer in the still night air was the spluttering of the lorry engine. He peered into the night and could just make out that the lorry was on fire and heading down the hill towards the rail crossing. He was about to rush inside and phone the fire brigade but felt compelled to watch its zigzag path. At the last moment the lorry veered, crashing head on, at about 40mph, into his signal box base. It dismantled the other side of the wooden building which immediately burst into flame. Holding onto the handrail for dear life he watched, open mouthed, as his big armchair slid slowly down, the now steeply sloping wooden floor, finally tipping into the inferno. His wood-burning stove was next spilling hot coals everywhere only adding to the flames. Dangling and clanging from the roof, the black metal pipes of the stove chimney were next and they collapsed noisily in front of him into the fire. Terrified but still hanging tightly onto the veranda handrail, he watched the inferno from the high side of his burning signal box.

As the flames took hold, the remnants of the signal box started to tilt towards the burning lorry fire, making the big man turn and half jump, half fall into the bushes alongside the track. Breaking his neck in the fall he lay in a grotesque, unnatural pose.

As the secret train sped through the dark countryside towards the level crossing unusual orange lights ahead caught George's eye and he sensitively applied the brakes. Relief filled his soul as the brakes took hold. This was the 10th night trial George and

Percy had been on since that fateful night and every time he touched the brakes he was still nervous.

Carston had asked specifically for the two of them to drive the trial train having seen how they handled the potential crisis near York. Neither Professor Jill nor Dr Carston were on board this evening, both having been present on the last five nights and dealing with some internal security crisis back at the depot in South Ruislip.

The train had been going through its trials beautifully when George first spotted the strange orange glow in the sky. Percy alerted the soldiers and George brought the train to a gentle stop about 50 yards from the burning signal box.

Three soldiers jumped down from the single carriage and ran along the track towards the signal box. Two stayed with the train. As soon as the three soldiers were at the signal box, men wearing black balaclavas appeared from the undergrowth on both sides of the train and started to board the engine. Their actions were aggressive and their intention was to take over from George and Percy. George was the gentler of the two and immediately held his hands in the air in surrender but this was Percy's train and no hooded train robbers were going to take it. Black balaclavas held no fear for Percy. He was used to street fighting in Glasgow and saw red.

As soon as he realised what was happening he lifted his shovel and one masked man after another, who had entered the cab from different sides, flew backwards out of the cab. The sickening noise of the shovel hitting their faces rang out in the night like a gong. Now George was back with Percy and in an effort to escape, put the big engine in reverse, starting to shunt backwards. The scene was chaos.

As George shunted the train backwards he saw the two young soldiers who had stayed, lying near the track, both with gunshot wounds in their chests. George felt sick. Four of the hooded men were still running alongside the engine, two each side, trying to catch up and board. A shot rang out then a second; George and Percy ducked down and Percy slammed the shovel into the face of the first of these hooded men as he tried to get on board. The scream as he fell backwards sent a shiver down George's spine.

A calm, almost surreal voice then said: "Ok, the fun's over. Slow the train down and let them get on board."

George and Percy slowly turned and there behind them standing on the coal at the top of the tender was a hooded man with a gun pointing straight at them. He couldn't miss. They looked at each other and George moved towards the controls.

"Slowly," said the gunman.

George lifted his hands as if in submission and moved cautiously towards the controls.

He pushed the control to the slow position and they all felt the lurch as the big engine slowed. This was the most responsive engine George had ever had the privilege to drive and he knew its limits especially after 10 nights of trials. As the gunman started his unsteady descent down the loose coal in the tender George slammed the lever forward and waited. Half a second passed, enough for the gunman to get his balance and start to take aim and then the backwards lurch of the engine flung him forward into the cab. Percy raised his shovel to dispatch him but George stopped him. There was no need. He was out cold. They pulled his hood to one side but neither of them recognised him.

The engine was now travelling backwards at top speed. Both George and Percy felt the threat was over and after tentative looks back at the puffing, hooded men who had now given up trying to catch them they slowed the train down. They turned to each other and grinned. Percy, still brandishing the dented shovel and bouncing with excitement, was the first to speak: "It's just like the old days back home." George laughed nervously.

Then a shot rang out and Percy slumped backwards holding his stomach.

The gunman who lay in the front of the cab with blood running from under his mask pointed the gun at George and said: "Stop the train now or I'll shoot you too."

George reluctantly pushed the lever forward allowing the train to slow down on its own. He then went straight over to tend to Percy and cradled his old friend's head. Blood flowed from the wound in his stomach and no matter how George tried to stem the flow with his free hand he couldn't. Percy's grimace of pain changed to a calm and then a smile. He struggled to speak; George lowered his head to hear: "We showed the bastards, eh George?" then he closed his eyes.

14
Two Glasses of Whisky

Jill and Carston chinked the crystal whisky glasses again, neither knowing exactly what to say as they tried to pass in the closeness of the dining room doorway. Jill looked up and put her free hand on Carston's jacket lapel as if to hold the moment. Absently, she stroked the coarse tweed material. He was a good six inches taller than her and in the dim, half-light of the flat she could hardly see into his dark eyes but could feel the stare of this handsome man. Her body shuddered with the same feeling when you know someone is looking at you but you're not sure where they are. His Bible black hair framed his face against the dull magnolia walls and Jill could smell the faint blackcurrant bouquet of wine on his breath, such was their closeness.

The mix of a late night, thick fog outside, warm inside, dim lighting, heady wine with the meal, an unplanned physical closeness and a peaty, 15-year-old Bowmore malt whisky unlocked the secured doors of sense and reason and she closed her eyes stretching up to be kissed.

Carston was breathing heavily looking into her eyes. His mind flashed back to finding himself watching her from behind his desk. He watched as she undertook the most menial of tasks. He found himself wondering what she was wearing beneath her corporate suit and his eyes traced the curves of her shape with the precision of a draughtsman's pencil. When in overalls, she was even more appealing as the sloppiness of the fit made her even more alluring. His free hand gently brushed away a curl of black hair from her forehead and his pursed lips started the downward journey to meet half way with hers.

The jangling telephone shocked them both out of the moment.

"What? Say that again," Carston listened intently to the news from the South Ruislip Depot and then repeated it as much to let it sink in as to inform Jill.

"Two soldiers dead. Percy dead. Oh no, not Percy. Is George OK?"

"In hospital? Will he be alright?"

"A signal box burnt to the ground and the signalman dead?"

"What about the train?"

"Ransacked?"

Jill relieved Carston of his drink and put them both down. There were follow-up questions: "Were, when, who, what did they want?"

He replaced the receiver and turned to her.

"You heard?"

"Some," she said
"Percy's dead. Shot."

"I'm sorry," she said and stroked his arm. Carston and the railway crew had become good friends over the last two weeks of trials and Jill had also become fond of both characters, George and Percy.

Jill and Carston had been bounced back to reality in an instant. They ordered another engine to be fired up and a new crew to be brought into the depot. They donned their coats and unlike the tipsy, playful couple that entered the flat 20 minutes earlier, two thoughtful, stone cold sober engineers left the flat in stunned silence.

15
Together at Last

On the platform, Celia dropped her two heavy cases and flung her arms around Carston's neck. She hugged him for all she was worth. He returned the hug and kissed her with a passion only known to newlyweds. Both were oblivious to the streams of people walking past them carrying cases and valises along the platform. Their kiss lasted until the last passenger had exited the platform and the only people left were railway staff who sensitively, ignored the pair. Carston and Celia eventually walked hand in hand out of the station and hailed a taxi to take them to his flat in West London.

Once inside, Carston showed her around the sparsely furnished flat and flung her suitcases next to their rickety three-quarter bed. Celia turned her nose up at the faded patchwork quilt on the bed saying that it reminded her of a care home! She tut-tutted at the ancient, tilting wardrobe with a badly fitting door, memories of her grandmother's, mothballed home. But by far the worst discovery of all was the set of brushes and cracked hand mirror sitting on the kidney shaped dressing table in their bedroom. She could never, ever, have dreamt of using any of them. The dressing table set, each item embroidered on the back with flying ducks, reminded her of her great aunt's kidney shaped dressing table with its three mirrors and accompanying rose design curtains. She had hated them then and she hated them now.

However, she squealed with delight when he led her into the tiny dining room where dinner was laid for two, complete with tall, thin, red candles adorning the centre of the table. She turned, launching herself at him and wrapped her arms around his neck again so tightly, saying with such feeling: "I've missed you so much darling."

Carston lifted her off the ground still in a hug position, carried her back into the bedroom and laid her gently on the bed. Celia resisted his advances by rolling off the bed the other side, insisting she needed a bath after her long journey. While she hunted for her silk dressing gown in one of the bursting suitcases, Carston dutifully went into the bathroom, turned on the huge, peeling, chrome, hot tap which spluttered a few times then cascaded water noisily into the deep bath - a deep, white, roll-top, freestanding bath with cast iron, lion claw feet. A bath, complete with a stain of verdant green tracing a line from the cold tap all the way down to the plughole from generations of dripping. A bath built in the last century for at least two occupants.

Carston reached for the blue, bath salts from the window sill and duly sprinkled the only ones that were loose from the container that was probably more of an ornament than for the use of guests. Eventually, when the bath was about a quarter full, steam started to rise from the surface of the water despite the coffin-cold, enamelled bath.

With her hair tied back and wearing her honeymoon silk dressing gown, Celia pushed open the bathroom door to be met by a wall of steam that smelled of old roses with a hint of old lavender: "It's just like a sauna in here and smells like a tart's boudoir," she joked.

Reaching for her he asked: "And how, may I ask, would you know what a tart's boudoir smells like?"

"Well it's just like I would imagine it would be. And how, may I ask, do you know what a tart's boudoir smells like to be able to question me?"

Wriggling out of his grasp she announced to his obvious disappointment:

"Anyway, you're not stopping in this tart's boudoir."

And with that she playfully pushed him out of the bathroom and closed the door.

Ten minutes later he quietly re-entered the bathroom carrying a bottle of champagne and two champagne flutes. He wore only a broad smile. She opened her eyes to see him placing the glasses on the little marble topped table next to the bath. She tried gathering the sparse bath bubbles to cover her modesty but to no avail, the movement of the water making the bubbles disappear the quicker.

Still new to married life, she was hugely embarrassed and protested until he laid a kiss lightly on her lips that tasted of champagne. Her embarrassment melted and she kissed him back. Carston raised her shoulders out of the warm water and shuffled her forward in the expansive bath. He then slid in behind her, wriggling one of his long legs down each side and gently pulled her backwards so she lay back on his chest. He kissed the top of her head and she wrapped his broad arms around her. There they lay, cocooned in a rosy champagne glow of being together; all the problems of the start of their married life behind them. Tonight they were together, tonight they were man and wife, tonight they would be one.

Carston gently wafted water over her exposed shoulders to keep her warm and blew in her ear when he felt she was beginning to get so cosy she could easily have drifted off to sleep. He nuzzled his nose into her soft hair and she playfully bit the back of his hand. With the champagne weaving its magic spell he suddenly pulled the plug out of the bath with his big toe and helped her to her feet. Stepping out first he pulled a soft, newly purchased, huge white bath towel from the noisy church-sized radiator and wrapped it around her like a baby. Her eyes were bright with anticipation and she felt loved. He had never felt so in love. Carston wrapped himself in an equally big white towel and the two of them, hand in hand made their way to the bedroom.

***

It must have been after midnight when they rose from the dinner table having laughed and drank wine throughout the meal. Carston had gone to great lengths to ensure that dinner was a mixture of all her favourites.

Celia left the room returning from the bedroom carrying the music box. She set it on the arm of the huge settee just as she had in the hotel in York and wound the brass key. He sat alongside her and tucked her under his arm in a cuddle. When the first tune had finished Celia rummaged in the little drawer, swapped to the second barrel then to the next until she had played them all. All that is, except the one that had a strange tune.

She loaded the odd barrel into the music box and they listened together.

"No idea," he said, "I've never heard the tune before. It's as though it's being played at the wrong speed. Can you change the speed?"

They examined the box and came to the same conclusion she had found earlier that there was only one speed.

"Strange," said Carston, "maybe it's from a different music box. "Try the barrel upside down," which they tried and found the barrels could only go in one way.

"Play it again please?"

Celia played it again and the two of them listened intently.

Carston drew a stave complete with a treble clef on his napkin: "Do you remember this from your school days? 'FACE spells Face In The Space' and the stave lines follow the saying, 'Every Good Boy Deserves Fruit'. We had it hammered into us by our religious studies teacher called Holy Joe who also tried to teach us the recorder. We disparagingly used to call them phlegm pipes." Celia reeved her nose up at the thought and he laughed out loud to himself at the memory.

"If you mark the strange notes from the music box on a music stave on my napkin," said Carston thoughtfully, "there's one 'a' on its own, then one 'd' followed by four 'd's, then an 'f' followed by nine 'f's and a single f, then an 'a' followed by 28 'a's. It's all a bit monotonous isn't it?"

"I've listened to it lots of times and can't recognise any tune," said Celia yawning, "I'm off to bed, it's been one very long day for me." And with that she yawned again and headed for the bathroom. Carston agreed screwing up his incomprehensible napkin but on his way to the bathroom opened his brief case and pulled out a clean sheet of paper. Intrigued he settled down in the big armchair drew another stave and wound the music box up again.

a

d   d ddd

f   fffffffff f

a   aa aaaaaaaaa a   aaa   aaaaaaa   aaaaaa

"Goodnight," she called.
Carston jumped up out of his trance, apologised and went into the bathroom.

"More tea?" Celia asked, leaning over the breakfast table followed with, "what shall we do today? We have the rest of today and all of tomorrow before we go back to work. Let's not waste a minute."

Carston smiled and shot her a look that said it all.

"You're terrible," she admonished and with that she playfully threw all of his papers from the previous night into the air and climbed onto his knee at the table like a little girl. He in turn pulled at her dressing gown cord and buried his head in her soft chest. Celia held his head as tight as she could against her body never wanting him to let him go. Awkwardness at the untidy breakfast table drove them to move to more comfortable surroundings and before she could protest she was lying on the bed with her dressing gown only partially covering her body.

16
Everyday Work

Carston worked harder and harder to push his invention beyond its limits. The trials so far had been successful but his belief was that he had only scratched the surface of a conventional locomotive's performance. Until his research, progress on steam efficiency had been pedestrian to say the least. There had been only incremental advances while Carston's ambition was for conceptional leaps forward. He found himself arguing for more and more money for spares, for extensions to nonsensical deadlines imposed by bureaucrats who saw only pound notes, not progress. Bureaucrats, whose myopic vision could be measured in days and weeks, whereas Carston's inventions would alter the face of steam locomotion for decades to come.

Conversely Professor Jill handled the politicians and the bureaucrats with considerably more skill than Carston. Her charm and knowledge advanced his cause far further than his head-on technique which, on occasions, made him feel slightly impotent. What Jill struggled with was the ineptitude of the planners of the rail network across the whole country. She could not comprehend how a country with the UK's level of prosperity was incapable of planning a strategic network to alleviate the overcrowded roads and give easy access to the country's coal and steel wealth. She was used to working in countries with only one per cent of the UK's GDP who, despite all their problems, saw the necessity of a coherent rail network.

Exasperation with politicians, on occasions, ended with Carston blowing his top and Jill having to calm the situation with her more grounded approach.

Celia, on the other hand, worked long hours in her antiseptic world, trying to help the endless queue of parents who were desperate for miracles for their children. She worked with lazy children who had learned to do just enough to satisfy their parents with painfully slow progress and also she worked with amazing kids, with larger than life personalities, who had no idea that they even had a disadvantage. She worked with genuinely slow to learn kids whose parents were highly embarrassed by their offspring not being as bright as other kids and with some dysfunctional parents who just didn't care.

However, every family that came to see her were given the same level of attention and love as every other family and despite their differences and all the obstacles, she moved every child forward. Maybe just a little, but forward all the same. And when the progress was painfully slow it hurt her deep inside and she had to keep returning to her original notes on the child to remember where they were on their first appointment with her. This gave her the impetus to redouble her efforts and research the very latest paediatric techniques from all over the country.

Her dedication and successes were beginning to become recognised. Slowly at first and only locally, but gradually her methods were being talked about by consultants and difficult cases were being referred directly to her. This acknowledgement gave her a huge sense of satisfaction. A satisfaction that this young woman from way up north in Fort William was turning the heads of the great and good in the paediatric world, but even more important for her was the progress of the children and their delight in their own achievement.

17
Disturbed Nights

A lazy day walking around Ruislip's Lido and an afternoon picnic made an idyllic day for both of them. That evening Carston and Celia ventured out to an Italian restaurant for dinner and took the remains of the second bottle of Chianti home to finish the evening in style.

Playing buses in bed for closeness pre-empted their deep, well-earned sleep.

At 3am Carston found himself wide-awake. He wriggled from her grasp and made his way back into the lounge.

As an avid crossword solution seeker the music box intrigued him beyond all reason.

"It might not be letters at all," he mumbled to himself, "it could be numbers or a mix of numbers and letters." And he wrote out the score of music followed by other combinations.

a..... a word beginning with the letter a

d...... a word beginning with d, followed by a 1 and a 3

f........ a word beginning with f, followed by a 9 and a 3 and a 1

a......a word beginning with a, followed by a 2 then a 9 then a 1, a long gap then a 3 then a 7 then a 6.

By 4am his eyes had grown heavy and he pushed the papers away. It made no sense. Perhaps it was just a tune, maybe a test barrel. Time for bed again.

The morning soon came despite his sub-conscious having been at work all night. He went to the kitchen and made tea for both of them. Celia stretched herself awake after he deliberately bumped into her side of the bed. Carston proceeded to climb in on her side pushing her off her warm spot to which she protested sleepily. They tumbled about playfully until the tea was nearly cold and delighted in, early morning, eyes closed, newlyweds, sleepy sex.

Over breakfast they mulled again over the music box and its contents. Carston retrieved the papers from the previous night and pored over them again.

A word beginning with the letter a.

A word beginning with the letter d, followed by a 1 and a 3.

A word beginning with the letter f, followed by a 9 a 3 and a1.

A word beginning with the letter a, followed by a 2 then a 9 then a 1 a long gap then a 3 then a 7 then a 6.

He wrote the letters differently.

a

d 13

f 931

a 291 376

"The last one could be a grid reference," said Celia.

"What do you know about grid references?" asked Carston with more surprise in his voice than intended.

"I didn't just sit around in Scotland drinking whisky and eating haggis," she admonished him. "I was in the Girl Guides for five years. Thinking back though I was in the Guides for five years because there was nothing else to do! Absolutely nothing," she said mournfully, reflecting back on those long evenings of working towards Guide badges.

"You know you could be right, let's see where it is on the map."

"It's a little place called Hucknall in Nottinghamshire. I've never heard of it, you?"

"Nope."

"What about the d?"

"Could it be distance? 13 miles? 13 yards could it be?"

"The f?

"Friday?"

"So according to you, Brains," she joked, "we now have the place, Hucknall in Nottinghamshire, we have the day Friday and it is 13 somethings from there."

***

They both decided the music box was becoming more of a burden than a fabulous wedding present, so decided to put it out of sight for a while to focus on enjoying their short time together. The day was spent doing nothing. Having morning coffee and afternoon tea and chatting like an old married couple and planning their ideal house in the country. They decided it had to have wisteria tumbling over the front porch, a rickety gate, orderly raised beds for vegetables with straight paths for him and a riot of all sorts of colourful flowers in the cottage borders for her, full of scents and smells of the country. And a herb garden. They both agreed the cottage had to have a herb garden.

Children, two or three or four, she couldn't decide, would play on swings fitted to the bough of an old apple tree and they would have lots of friends around to play in their big garden. Chickens would roam freely and their two Labrador dogs, one gold and the other black, would sleep in the conservatory.

All in all they planned their perfect life together. Dinner was by candlelight again in the tiny dining room and the day ended as it had begun, as close as any two people could get.

Suddenly, Carston sat bolt upright in bed. He woke Celia with a start: "Where did the music box originally come from?"

"What are you talking about?" said a sleepy little voice, "stop thinking about the blessed music box will you. We're supposed to be on our honeymoon. Snuggle up to me and go back to sleep. Let's think about it in the morning."

"I've just thought of something. Just tell me where you bought it and I promise I'll let you go back to sleep.

Please, just humour me for a little while. Just tell me where you bought it."

"London, somewhere in London: an antique shop. I just happened to come across it when I was a bit lost. A dingy back street place with surprisingly few things for sale in it now I come to think of it," Celia replied between yawns. "Now can we go back to sleep?"

"Did they say where the music box originated?"

"No, the sales girl wasn't very bright and when she went to check if she could even sell it to me, she got an awful telling off from the owner for disturbing him. He was a really short, nasty man with a funny thick foreign accent, so, no I don't know where it originally came from. Please can I now go back to sleep?"

"I think the music box probably originated in Germany, Switzerland or Austria. Therefore the letters would be for German words not English words at all. Look I'll show you."

"Oh no, not now," she pleaded. But he was already in his dressing gown and heading for the door.

"Darling, come back to bed," was her exasperated plea, but in the short time she had known him she realised he was single-minded in the extreme. Celia, still with eyes still closed tight, reached for her dressing gown and grudgingly followed him into the sitting room. There she found him, poring over the previous night's papers. She slumped down alongside him elbows on the table her hands cupping her sleepy head.

"You see, d in German could be Datum, the date. 1:3 i.e. 1st March"

"A could be the grid reference just as you said and the German word could be angriffsziel meaning target. Whatever is in Hucknall in Nottinghamshire is the target. I don't know of anything in Hucknall of value. In fact I think I've read somewhere they call it 'Mucky 'ucknall' because of the collieries in that area. Anyway, the f could be frist which is German for deadline. 09. 31 am and the other a could be abbau."

Carston went quiet. Quiet enough to completely wake Celia by the seriousness of his tone.

"Where did you say you bought it?"

"I bought it in a tiny antique shop in a back street in London. It was run by a crabby owner who shouted at the sales girl who served me." And then she said very slowly, "He had a very strong foreign accent. Why, what does abbau mean?" she asked, now completely awake.

"Abbau in German means 'complete destruction'."

They both became cold at the same time.

Carston read out all of the bits together.

"On March 1ˢᵗ at 9.31am at these Hucknall coordinates there is to be complete destruction."

"What should we do with this information?"

"We need to get it to the MoD. Right now!"

"Are you sure, really sure. We're not going to be seen as weirdos?"

They quickly dressed, gathered all of his working papers and left into the night.

At the MoD they were met by a young officer who was not going to disturb any senior officer with a cock and bull story about a coded message in a music box, no matter what! He told them they could wait in the waiting room till the morning or come back at 8am. It was 3.30am.

However, he did start to waver when Carston asked if the colonel in charge was a man called Atherton-Swan who he had been in school with. The young officer became nervous at this connection, eventually offering to contact the senior officer by phone.

Colonel Atherton-Swan had always been a heavy sleeper and normally nothing would have roused him, but a call of nature meant he was up and busy when the phone rang.

Hearing who was at the front gatehouse, he reluctantly dressed and made his way down to meet with Carston and Celia.

There were the normal pleasantries and he led them into a side room.

"Now what's all this about, Prestwick old Chap?"

Carston slowly explained about the music box and as he was recounting the story he could see Atherton-Swan's eyes start glazing over, believing this to be just another '1938 enemy everywhere' story. That was until he mentioned 'complete destruction'. He was mildly interested but when Carston mentioned Hucknall all Hell broke loose.

Senior officers were summoned, guards were doubled on the outside of the building and all Carston's working papers on the code were taken away for scrutiny.

"Where's this music box now?" asked a now, very awake, Atherton-Swan.

"Back at the flat."

"I'll send two men with you to get it. Bring it straight back here. Don't talk to anyone, do you understand?"

"So you think this is really a message or an instruction for someone?"

"Can't be too careful, old chap, can't be too careful," said Atherton-Swan with an agitated but non-committal air.

"What's so important about the 1st of March and Hucknall then?"

"Only the meeting of all the friendly heads of Europe to view Britain's latest aeroplane and Hucknall is the Rolls-Royce engine-testing centre for the UK. It's there they've been testing the new aircraft engines. Apparently, it's a world-beater. My squad have been seconded to travel up to guard this Nottinghamshire aircraft engine-testing unit in a few days' time. There will be all sorts of demonstrations to show the heads of Europe that we are more than ready for any sort of war, if it comes. We'll have superiority in the air all over Europe."

Celia and Carston were escorted home by two soldiers to bring back the music box. What they found back at their flat was complete chaos. Their clothes had been strewn all over the floor of the flat and their possessions had been turned out of all of the drawers. The bed had been turned upside down and the kitchen ransacked. Celia was in floods of tears when she discovered her pendant and purse were missing and said a little prayer of thanks that she had put her rings on before they left in such a hurry. Carston was upset when he discovered his silver fountain pen, a special present from his father, had been taken from his brief case.

The music box was also missing.

The four of them searched high and low for the box but soon came to the conclusion that it had also been stolen. One of the soldiers was on the phone like a shot. Several minutes later he came off the phone saying: "We are to return to the MoD. You sir are to ring the police and treat this as a normal burglary. We don't want to make a fuss to alert the thieves that we have any understanding of the music box's significance. When the police arrive please don't make any reference to what you have discovered about the music box. Treat this as a normal burglary."

The two soldiers left through the back door and Carston dutifully phoned the police. Two hours later a lone Bobby arrived on his bicycle, took some notes, explained he was dealing with a spate of burglaries at the moment and with misguided cheerfulness doubted they would get any of their possessions back. Once the Bobby had gone, a dismayed and thoroughly dejected Celia and a very angry Carston began the big clean up.

18
The Music Box is Returned

For the first time, in a long time, Hans and the weasel man felt reasonably comfortable entering the little antique shop. This time there seemed to be a slightly more cheerful tone to the bell. But despite its welcome there at the back of the dimly lit shop, like a guard dog in the dark corners of a kennel, sat the shop owner, glowering over frameless spectacles. His demeanour hadn't changed, hadn't changed that is since last time, until he saw they were carrying a bag. Standing up, he waved his hand for the bag without saying a word. The two men noticed the shopkeeper's right eye twitch in anticipation, while he waited impatiently for them to walk across the shop.

Carefully he retrieved a rectangular object from the bag that was wrapped neatly in a thick white fluffy bath towel that smelled of old roses and old lavender.

Unfolding the towel with great care he instantly recognised the music box and stroked the marquetry lid as if he were holding the hand of a long lost lover.

He couldn't believe his recent misfortune at its loss and it still pained him to think of the consequences of not retrieving it. The music box had been delivered during a busy Saturday afternoon complete with an outrageous price tag to complete its cover. If it did fall into the wrong hands its heavily coded contents were intended to confuse and misguide the casual observer. But it mustn't become lost at any price. Too much depended on the message getting through to the sleeping cell of undercover operatives. March 1st was all-important.

The music box had travelled across the whole of Europe with other antiques in the care of a man only referred to as Courier. Courier had no knowledge of its contents. Some of the antiques, once through England's Customs and Excise officers, were of no value to Courier and discarded, other small items arrived with the music box for authenticity. Confident that its outrageous price would dissuade potential buyers, Courier left it on the owner's desk in the shop while he and the owner went into the back office for privacy.

Meanwhile, the newly-appointed shop assistant was showing a young lady around the shop trying to advise her on a present for her husband-to-be. Everything had either been too big or not quite right and she was fast running out of time until the bride-to-be spotted the music box on the desk. Not quite sure if she should sell the music box, the new assistant knocked on the back office door and before she had been able to speak was told on no account was she to disturb them again. The door was slammed shut in her face. A lot of cash changed hands and the bride-to-be left the shop delighted with her purchase, despite being considerably the poorer.

The sale had been a complete disaster for the shop owner. The music box had travelled right across Europe carrying its coded message and as soon as it was put in his hands it had disappeared without trace. Raised voices echoed around the shop. Courier was beside himself with rage. The assistant, who was in floods of tears, was sacked on the spot but after consideration was instructed to stay and talk to other employees of the shop owner. This is when Hans and the weasel man had been brought in to interview her with a view to recovering the box.

Then she was sacked.

The disappearance of the music box had led to a very anxious time for the shop owner and his huge relief at its return was obvious. Once reacquainted, he immediately felt inside the box for the drawer for the barrels. He took them out very carefully, one by one and set them on the desk in a neat row. The strange barrel was, of course, the last to come out. He examined it under the green shaded desk lamp, then carefully inserted it into the workings of the music box. Slowly, winding the brass key till it stopped turning, he settled down in his seat to listen. He was oblivious to his curious audience.

The second time he played the tune he wrote down a series of numbers just as Carston had. His head nodded in time with the notes and he drummed out the beats with his finger. As he interpreted the code in his head his face turned to a smile, as he understood the message. Hans and weasel man just looked at each other completely perplexed by the strange sounds coming from the box.

"You're sure nobody saw you?"

"Sure."

"You're sure they will think it's just a normal burglary?"

"Yes."

"Did you take other things as well?"

"Of course," and they showed him the pendant, her purse and Carston's silver pen.

"You've done well. You'll be well rewarded."
A nervous call was put in to the Motherland to let them know, 'their gift had been returned.'

19
A Surprise Meeting

In the Ear, Nose and Throat Clinic, Celia was kneeling down opposite a tousled haired little boy and playing a game with him. She was holding an inflated yellow balloon between their faces and making b,b,b,b,b,b,b sounds into the balloon. The air in the balloon enhanced the b sound and the little boy, who had never spoken, smiled with surprise and delight at the feeling of the vibrations on his face. Celia did it several times and then gestured it was his turn. He held the balloon carefully, one hand on either side and after heaps of encouragement tried to do what Celia had done. There was lots of blowing and dribbling with eyes shut tight in a desperate desire to show her he could do it.

After a while, Celia stopped the little boy from trying so hard and was about to take the balloon away and try something else when he snatched the balloon back and pushed it into her face and took up the position again. More blowing and much more dribbling and this time tears started to show in his sad eyes at the little boy's self-perceived inadequacy. Celia was willing him to be successful and praying for even the tiniest squeak. The little boy's face became redder and redder. Then he made the tiniest b,b sound, snatched the balloon away and gave her the biggest grin through his tear-wet, little face. Celia crawled over and hugged the little boy as tears also streamed down her face. She told him he was the most fantastic, amazing little boy she had ever known. The little boy fairly glowed with her encouragement.

"You were born to do this," said a voice from behind her.

She looked up and saw Austin McGregor standing behind her in a white, junior doctor's coat with a stethoscope around his neck. He was broader than she remembered, he was shorter than she remembered but he was just as handsome, perhaps even more handsome.

Celia stood up and blushed as she wiped away the tears with her handkerchief. She signalled for the delighted little boy to go over to a heap of toys as a reward for his b,b sound.

Now in control Celia spoke: "Well, as I live and breathe, Austin McGregor. I thought you would be in darkest Africa or some such place still travelling."

"I'm back. Do I get a hug after all this time then?"

"Do you deserve a hug?"

"I suppose not. However, could I buy you a drink for old time's sake?"

"Why?"

"You're not making this easy for me are you Celia?"

"Why should I?" she snapped. "You left me to come to London on my own. On my very own. Me, Celia, Specky Four Eyes, on my own. I'd never been further than the High Street in Fort William! Let alone London. Me, London? My family told me there would be dragons on the other side of Hadrian's Wall, and not to trust Englishmen for they were after one thing only, and to be very careful for the English had still never forgiven us for their defeat at Bannockburn."

Austin winced at the tirade: "Sorry, I just wasn't ready."

"Nor was I!" Celia snapped again. She was nearly in tears at the painful memory of the station at Fort William with her luggage already loaded onto the train and all she wanted to do was to go home with her distraught mother. She had never felt so alone.

Celia was now on the high ground. A place she had never been with Austin McGregor before.

"Coffee?" he suggested.

"The coffee's diabolical here. You can buy me lunch instead. one o'clock outside the main entrance," and with that she turned and went over to the little boy to continue his therapy.

***

At one o'clock on the dot Celia stood outside the hospital entrance, in the rain, wondering why on earth people smoked. She squashed herself against the grubby wall to stay out of the rain but the smell of tobacco smoke was heavy in the air and the number of cigarette ends around her feet was legion. There must be a link, she thought, between the huge increase in respiratory patients and smoking. Some of the children she treated had, what could only be described as, smoker's coughs and as soon as she met the parents she knew why. They reeked of stale tobacco smoke and couldn't wait to get out of her office to light up. There had to be an impact on the children as passive smokers she thought.

She decided to give Austin five more minutes and then go. She wouldn't wait a moment longer. She couldn't understand why she had agreed to meet him after all this time. She wondered if she just wanted to gloat, her being a paediatrician and him still a junior doctor? Or was it that she was no longer Specky-

Four-Eyes any more but a worldly woman who was married to a successful Doctor of Engineering and he was just the same? Or was it she still held a candle for him even after all this time?

She allowed herself to drift and think. He was just the same; same engaging eyes, same powerful frame and same wonderful smile. Celia flitted between excitement and anger. She still smarted at being left to come to London on her own. But as a result of coming on her own she had become a confident, assertive woman. She was now comfortable with her lot and reasonably settled in her new married life. Soon she and Carston would be buying a house in the country and then there would be babies, lots of babies. Her world would then be complete.

She thought about Carston. Although she would never admit it she didn't like her husband working so closely with another woman, it made her slightly uncomfortable. Carston had initially talked about how well they worked together and how much more experience she had than him, but that had reduced to a level where he hardly mentioned her now. Celia didn't know which was worse. She countered the argument in her head by remembering that she worked with lots of male doctors so a level of trust was needed on both sides. She imagined all newly marrieds initially felt this way with their spouses working closely with members of the opposite sex and felt the feelings would pass.

The time was five minutes past 1pm, now. Three more minutes and she was definitely going to go. It was raining more heavily by now and her umbrella was being buffeted by the wind and rain. She pulled her raincoat tightly around her and remembered the bad weather up in Scotland, the incessant rain of Fort William. She remembered not wanting to wear her raincoat for school as it wasn't fashionable and here she was, in London, pleased to have bought one for herself out of her first wage. Her mother had laughed when she told her.

The enjoyment of her school days had been mixed, but her fondest memories were of the School Reviews organised by the 6th form pupils from both schools. Everyone played a role. Austin always played the lead roles and had always been a hit. The biggest rounds of applause was when he came back on the stage at the end for the final bow. She had been in costumes or make-up or some back-stage role and received only polite, token applause in comparison. The biggest applause was always for Austin. Then, she had just been pleased to be part of something he was in.

When the teacher who did Austin's make-up went home sick and Celia had been told to take over she nearly died. She had never been that close to him before. Her hands were trembling as she tried to apply eye shadow around his dark eyes. She could feel his breath on her cheeks; she could feel his pulse as she applied foundation cream down his throat and onto his curly chest hair. Twice, just to make sure, she applied the cream, stroking down from his temples over his high cheekbones across the teenage stubble on his cheeks and chin and down to the limit of his costume. She dreamt about it for weeks and weeks after, her within kissing distance of the most handsome boy in the High School and him rehearsing his lines with his eyes shut tight. She shuddered even now at the thought of smoothing foundation cream over his lean face…

Then a drop of cold rain ran down her neck and brought her forward seven years with a jolt. She turned and headed, in temper, back into the revolving door and the hospital. She wasn't going to wait a second longer. As she was shuffling into the hospital through the revolving door so Austin was shuffling out of the hospital waving frantically at her. Celia noticed him at the very last moment and continued in the revolving door to return back outside to join him. Austin was also committed and returned back inside the hospital.

The two of them laughed at the nonsense situation and Austin gestured through the doors for her not to move but stay exactly where she was. He joined her outside in the rain. This time he kissed her on the cheek before she could protest.
Celia shuddered inside.

"Hi. So sorry I'm late. Got involved in a really interesting bowel operation, couldn't drag myself away."

"Well, how special do I feel? You find a bowel op more interesting than lunch with me? I think I'll go back around the revolving door again."

"No, I didn't mean that, I meant....well, never mind. Lyon's Corner House?"

"Fine," and with that he slid his arm inside hers and dropped in beside her to share her umbrella. They chatted on the way to the teashop as though they had never been apart. So much for her plan of aloofness and distance from him she thought to herself. Inside the teashop they spotted an elderly couple about to leave and made their way across the crowded room to the vacated table. Celia hung her wet coat on an adjacent hat stand and joined him. He stood and held the chair for her as she sat down. He was still charming she thought and found herself wondering if Carston would have held the chair for her to sit down. She decided, probably not. They squeezed onto the tiny table and ordered tea, some tomato soup and warm lavender scones for afters.

They covered the difficult topic of what happened immediately after they went their separate ways and, once over, any underlying tensions evaporated. Austin talked about his travels across Africa and of the adventures he had been involved with and when it was her turn Celia told him about Carston and the wedding and the train incident. Within minutes they were reminiscing about the school days and bringing each other up to date about mutual friends and teachers. The atmosphere was comfortable; there was frequent laughter and the nature of the geography of the table setting ensured a closeness that neither could have engineered better.

They laughed at the memories of the School Reviews and the subject of make-up was raised. Celia admitted how nervous she had been when she had to make him up and he unexpectedly shared how excited he had been by her closeness. Celia blushed. Austin admitted he had to keep rehearsing his lines to stop himself from reaching up and kissing her as she applied his eyeliner and he couldn't even start to tell her what was happening to other parts of his body when she was rubbing cream on his neck and chest. Celia blushed even redder.

Seven years on and each now two hundred years older it was OK to share their feelings openly. Celia found he had his hand on her arm as he told her how he felt about her back in their school days and she in turn shared how she had been kept awake at night thinking about him. They laughed at the silliness of the school crushes but secretly each was trembling inside. She even admitted it was her who had stolen his school scarf and kept it all through her studies.

"Why didn't you say anything?"

"Why didn't you?"

Celia felt excited that the conversation was straying into dangerous territory and Austin felt gutted that he was just three weeks too late.

They walked back to the hospital dancing around the puddles together and laughing.

20
Back in the Board Room

"What? One signal box man dead, two British soldiers dead, a footplate man dead, four of our men in private hospitals having facial surgery and a train driver in a trauma clinic. What in Hell's name happened?" The major was standing at his desk with both clenched fists resting in the table.

Pickard squirmed in his seat.

"Well sir, the plan was to stop the train at the road crossing and reverse it back half a mile or so to take a look at the engine. Just as we discussed sir," said Pickard reminding the major of his involvement in the plan.

"Who was in charge?"

"I was."

Pickard's head wound completely escaped the major's notice.

"It must have been carnage. What in God's name happened?" Pickard knew he was completely dispensable and needed to align the major with the disaster as closely as he could. Implication was the name of the game now.

"I never reckoned on a big Scot with a death wish who was on the engine footplate. He put our four men in hospital with a coal shovel."

"A coal shovel? And all your people had guns?"

"Yes, all of OUR people had guns sir." The major ignored the subtle redistribution of blame and continued: "Anyway, what did Shawcross find out?"

"He examined the engine and found out that the train is fitted with a special continental smoke deflector and some other gadgets that he took photos of. We're waiting for them to be developed."

"Is that it? Is that it? God Almighty." The major looked up at the ceiling, his voice getting louder by the second. "Four men dead and all you can say is that we are waiting for a few snaps to be developed? Oh, that makes me feel better doesn't it? Boots the Chemist will process these snaps and then we can all have a good look at what is going to put us all out of business. Can't Shawcross tell us anything before that?"

"No sir, not at this time. He hasn't seen anything like it before."

"Bloody useless, bloody, bloody useless." Shaking his head the major muttered to himself: "I only hope this fiasco has been worth it." Then he turned on Pickard again: "Is there any possibility that this can be traced back to you? Anything at all? Anything left at the site? Any faces seen? Any word spoken?"

"No, nothing and it was all cleared up before even Shawcross was allowed anywhere near the engine. Nothing can be traced back to US sir."

"Bring me the photos and Shawcross as soon as they're ready, I want to know what we've been dealing with that's worth four deaths. And make sure the other directors don't find out about this."

Pickard suggested the Government would slap a 'D' notice on the incident so it's unlikely any of the directors would find out. He left without a word about his head wound.

Major Brown sat back heavily into his leather swivel chair assessing the cost of the exercise. Murder had never been part of his plan. It was something he had not even contemplated. It had come completely out of the blue. The financial value of competition-beating-train technology was astronomical and would run into hundreds of thousands of pounds of profit and Major Brown knew it would reposition the business and keep the shareholding wolverines off his back; but murder? Murder was the last thing he had expected.

Looking around the room he could feel the head shaking and tut-tutting of his predecessors scowling down at him, remonstrating their disapproval from their silent poses. It was more than he could bear so he lit a cigar and left the gloomy boardroom deep in thought.

21
A Date?

The date of the race had been fixed on 30th April. Carston and Jill worked on the engine taking it apart, testing every component and rebuilding it. Their night trials had been uneventful since the night Percy was killed, but their closeness did not go unnoticed by the other engineers.

They would regularly start a new project nearly at the end of a shift and rather than leave it incomplete, work late on into the night to complete.

Neither had planned the magnetism that drew them together. Carston found himself comparing Jill with Celia and how Jill was intellectually stimulating with an inexhaustible amount of international railway experience against, what originally had been charming stories of miniscule achievements of children with speech difficulties he now found slightly tedious. Jill and Carston's jokes became slightly more risqué and both pushed the boundaries a little further each day. Working in confined spaces they often found themselves squashed together unable to miss the smell of each other's soaps and shampoos.

Celia on the other hand was patient with Carston knowing the big race was approaching. Early on in their marriage she had spent careful time preparing the meals he favoured, but as the apologising telephone calls came thicker and faster, she found herself more often than not, eating alone. She comforted herself that this was just a temporary situation and after 30th April life would return to normal. When Carston did come home he was often so tired that he just wanted to collapse into bed and whereas this comment used to belie another meaning, now he meant exactly what he said and he was regularly asleep before she had even had time to brush her teeth.

In the lonely bed beside the rhythmic breathing of Carston, she often relayed to herself the events of the day. She had found herself watching to see if any white coat that came onto her department was Austin's and tried to stop feeling disappointed when it was one of the myriad of other doctors who all wore white coats.

Their lunch had been a strange occasion. He had seemed genuinely pleased to see her and at the start of lunch all she had done was to make him feel guilty for all of the ills of her stay in London. She even found herself boasting about her Carston and how important he was to the war effort and how he had guards around where he worked, so nationally critical was his work. But lunch had turned out to be very enjoyable, there was still a spark there and his comments about his schoolboy feelings for her had flattered her beyond her wildest dreams. When they parted after lunch he had held her arms and moved towards her to give her a peck on the cheek, she had not recoiled away despite being a married woman and all that.

Back in her department she was so cross with herself for the way she'd behaved towards him. She had been rude to him when they first met in her department and it would serve her right if he never saw her again. In a quiet moment Celia found herself idly flicking through the hospital telephone directory and her heart jumped a little when she saw his name and his telephone number.

Could she ring him? If she did have the courage, especially after last time, what would she say? What if he wasn't there? What message would she leave? Worse, what if he was there. What would she say? 'Would you like to start again?' No, that was too forward. 'How are you?' No that was too formal. 'Would you like lunch'? After last time he would probably say something like, 'No thanks, once bitten twice shy,' and she couldn't blame him. She sighed and then remembered she was married to a super guy who loved her dearly and there wasn't anything else in the world she wanted. They were going to live in a little house outside London, with wisteria over the front porch and have lots of babies.

She slammed the telephone directory shut and turned to attend to her next patient. Standing right behind her was Austin.

"Don't do that," she snapped at him.

Without speaking he turned and started to walk away. Celia rushed after him and caught his sleeve.

"I'm sorry. That was rude of me. Please come back into my office."
Austin hesitated not wanting to be rebuffed again.

"I promise I'll behave this time."

"I was just passing and wondered if you would like…"

"I'd love to."

"But you don't know what I'm going to ask."

"Lunch would be great."

"Perhaps you'll let me finish so I could ask you properly?"

"Sorry," and Celia fell silent, put her hands behind her back and looked at the floor like a little girl who has been naughty.

"Some of the junior doctors are having a drink after work tonight. Would you like to come with me? I'll introduce you to some of them; they're quite decent when you get to know them. I promise it won't be late as I have to be up really early tomorrow?"

Celia pondered. Carston had already told her he would be very late home and the prospect of spending another night eating on her own and re-reading Jane Eyre didn't appeal.

Celia looked down at her uniform and sensible shoes. Austin noticed and pre-empted the question.

"Most people will be in their uniforms and the doctors will still have stethoscopes hanging around their necks. You'll be fine."

"Thank you for the invitation. I'd love to go with you."

"See you outside at 6.00 then?"

***

The two of them entered the smoky pub on Sandringham Street and, true to Austin's word; many of the guests were still in uniform. As everyone seemed to be holding a drink Celia assumed, quite wrongly, that everyone had finished for the day, then why the white coats and stethoscopes?

"Drink?"

"Gin and tonic please."

"I'd sooner keep you a week than a fortnight," came the swift reply, "junior doctor's wages I'm on. Did you say a half of bitter?"

Quick as a flash Celia replied: "You can always tell the Scottish doctors 'first out of the taxi and last to the bar'." But Celia's reply was lost in the buzz of party noise as Austin made his way to the bar.

Austin, apart from the drinks, was the perfect host. He introduced her to some of his friends and colleagues who he regularly worked with. Celia for her part kept her wedding ring in sight all the evening and noticed all his female friends spotted it but said nothing. He called her a taxi promptly when she suggested it was time to leave and saw her safely inside. This time she allowed him to give her a slightly longer friendly peck on the cheek after thanking him for the invitation.
Inside the taxi she sighed.

22 The Major's Office

A gentle knock announced his secretary: "A Mr Hawk is here to see you Major Brown." For the second introductory sentence his secretary closed the door behind her and mouthed half the next sentence rather than say it out loud: "I think he's foreign," she whispered behind her hand.

"Hawk? Hawk? Do I know him?" asked the major quizzically, smiling inwardly at her old fashioned narrow mindedness.

"The gentleman said he felt sure you will see him. Apparently, you have some common friends. He mentioned a Mr James and a Lord Moger by name. Would you like me to tell him you are in a meeting and to make a proper appointment in, say a month's time?"

The names of Mr James and Lord Moger sent a shiver down the major's spine. These were not names he wanted to hear for a while.

"No, show him in I'll see what he wants."

Mr James and Lord Moger belonged to the same gentleman's club as the major and were ardent card players. The major believed his luck was about to change but was heavily into IOUs with both men.

Mr Hawk was shown into his office and sat down after shaking the major's hand.
His handshake was not the handshake of an accountant or teacher. It was the handshake of a man who regularly uses his hands to achieve what he wants. A handshake so firm that it left even an army major secretly wincing in pain.

"How can I help you Mr Hawk?"

The tall man in horn-rimmed glasses replied in a heavy German accent.

"Major Brown, I can think of 12,000 reasons how you can help me or rather help Mr James and Lord Moger."

£12,000 was the major's outstanding debt and just at this current moment in time gathering £12,000 was a complete impossibility.

"I need more time," he blustered, "tell them I will pay but I need time to liquidate some assets."

"Major Brown, you have no assets. I have researched your bank and your accountant. You are close to personal bankruptcy."

"How dare you look into my private affairs? What gives you the right to investigate me?" and with that the major stood up to position himself on higher ground.

"Sit down. You have no assets and cannot pay, so stop being pompous and listen. There may be a way."

"Your previous occupation was in security in the army was it not?"

"It was."

"And there are still people who you know who still work there?"

"Some."

"On the 1st of March there will be a delivery of aero engines for demonstration to the heads of governments from all over Europe. All I wish to know is which gate of the Hucknall site they will be delivered at. Here is £1,000 cash for you to use as you see fit."

At this point Mr Hawk tossed an envelope across the table to him. Major Brown fingered the envelope. This was more money than he'd handled in a very long time.

"£1,000 for information? You must be joking," said the major, pushing the envelope back.

"You didn't let me finish. This £1,000 cash is for you and the other £12,000 will be paid off on your behalf to Mr James and Lord Moger. A condition is that you say nothing about this conversation to anyone. Do you understand?"

The major sat down abruptly. He repeated the offer slowly to confirm it: "For the information of the gate the engines will be delivered at you will give me £1,000 cash and pay off all my debts to Mr James and Lord Moger?"

"Yes."

"How long have I got?"

"Two days."

"Two days? Two days? You must be mad. How can I get the information in two days, a week perhaps but not two days?"

"Then it's good day major," and with that Hawk rose, collected the envelope and headed for the door.

Before he reached the door the major had reconsidered and agreed to get the information for him and the envelope duly returned to him. The door closed behind Hawk.

The major snapped an instruction into the intercom: "Get my car around the front for me. As quickly as possible."

Two hours' driving later he arrived at what had been his old command town. He wondered if there was anyone left who would remember him. His favourite pub had been the Seven Stars in Hucknall and he made his way straight to it. The landlord had changed, so had the rest of the staff. He knew no-one. He bought a pint and a cheese sandwich and settled into a corner to decide how he was to retrieve the information about the delivery of the engines. He felt he could probably bluster his way into the army guardhouse as an old soldier and chat about the good old days when he was there. Or he could go to the army barracks and see if there was anyone he recognised. Trouble was that in today's age of pending war everyone was on high alert and looking for spies in every corner. Posters about, 'walls having ears' were everywhere. He was at the bar and just about to order another pint when someone touched his shoulder and asked at the same time: "Is it the major?"

He turned to see his old RSM standing stiffly behind him: "At ease sergeant-major ," he said: "No need for any of that stuff now. Pint?"

They sat back down in the corner of the pub and reminisced about the old days and some of the scams they had either been on or had to break. They were easy in each other's company as they always had been. After about five pints the major broached the subject of the RSM's current role.

The RSM explained he had been downgraded to corporal and was now on security duties on nights just through a bit of a misunderstanding with a 'Rupert' (officer) after a few pints. It wasn't like the old days when things were settled like men. Everything now had to go through the 'proper channels'. His pay had taken a huge knock too and with two daughters in university he was struggling to make ends meet.

The major pushed £100 across the table to him in 20s 'for old time's sake'. At first the ex-RSM refused, but when he flicked through the money and realised just how much it was and what a difference it would make he thanked him profusely.
The rest was easy.

Armed with the information the major needed he started the long drive home.

23 The Cell is Ready

In the back office of the antique shop the owner, Hawk and the two men who constituted the 'sleeping' cell, planned the next stage of their sabotage. Furnished with all the details they needed, it was now just a question of logistics. The right people, the right equipment, the right attitude and the consequences of their actions would set the British war effort back at least three years. More important, those heads of other governments who were wavering would capitulate and change allegiance if Britain's flying power was publicly seen to be impotent.

The cell was briefed, explosives were identified and the transport organised. All there was now to do was stay low and wait for the 1st of March.

24
Celia and the Party

On the phone Carston apologised to Celia but said that he would have to undertake trials of the engine all over the country to experience different weather conditions and different terrain of rail gradients. As such, he had been instructed not to communicate with anyone for a week till this phase of the work was completed, just as a precaution. He said he was sorry over and over again but it didn't help. After the call Celia cried and cried. This was not how she'd envisaged married life at all. They should be going to dinners together, they should be going to the theatre together, they should be inviting friends around for dinner. Not him on his own constantly at work with his silly train and her playing the good wife at home.

She did however, console herself in the knowledge that Austin and some of his friends were going to a ' finals are over, party' for some of the junior doctors. They had invited Austin and Celia to join them.

There hadn't been time to ask Carston if he minded her going, in their brief telephone call and even if she wanted to, now she couldn't, as there was no means of communicating with him, he'd made that very plain. At the end of the call and after he had said sorry, what seemed to him a hundred times, there had been an unfamiliar dismissal in his voice. A 'I have no choice in the matter' finality. A dismissal that she eventually interpreted, when she was in a more conciliatory mood, that was because there had been so much going on recently at the secret railway depot with the security breach and with the killing of Percy.

She admonished herself, she was being selfish and she should be more supportive for after the train race she felt sure life would return to normal. Normal, she queried of herself. What exactly was normal? Did she really want normal? Her parents' life? Was that what she wanted, was that normal? Definitely not! She would die of boredom with their routines. Lamb on Sunday, shepherd's pie on Monday, sausages on Tuesday, hot pot Wednesday, bacon, eggs and chips on Thursday and totally predictably fish on Friday. After savouring London for four years with its continental food and meal times, and wine with dinner every night, predictability was the last thing she yearned.

Celia conceded that what she had at this moment was not so very bad. She had a good job surrounded by like-minded, good fun doctors and nurses, a husband who said he loved her and who was heading for a place on his company's board of directors and the freedom to have a life of her own and enjoy herself when he was away. Celia uncorked a bottle of wine and settled down to while the evenings away till the night of the party.

Eventually it arrived and after trying on every dress from her meagre wardrobe she decided upon a sensible, high-necked dress with court shoes that only had a slight heel. Make-up was administered sparingly so as not to give the wrong message and scent was omitted completely from her preparations.

She looked long and hard at herself in the mirror. What message was she trying to portray to the other party goers?

Was it, 'I'm happily married so don't even try', or 'I'm married so it's unlikely to go anywhere', or 'I've an open mind', or 'I'm very free', or, 'just tonight, I'm free'?

Her clothes said 'I'm married, so it's unlikely to go anywhere' and that was enough to give her a heightened sense of risk. The fact she was going to a party with another man was a secret in what had become her husbandless, humdrum life. The fact that she was going with someone upon whom she had a three-year teenage crush was deliciously secret and also very exciting.

Anyway, she argued with herself, where's the harm? It was just one evening with some friends. It was perfectly innocent. It was to do with work. As some of the junior doctors had been seconded to her department in her position she would be expected to go. There was a protocol to follow. It was her job.

Anyway she was going!

The taxi duly arrived and she read out the address. She and Austin had agreed to meet at the party as he lived in the other direction. The journey was shorter than expected and she stepped out of the taxi into a normally quiet cul-de-sac. However, one house was bouncing with noise. People with drinks spilled out into the front garden, all the windows were open and music blared from every door and window. Before even going inside the house she felt in a party mood, she couldn't help it, such was the magnetic atmosphere.

Celia picked her way between the noisy and colourful partygoers and made for the drinks table in the kitchen. She placed a half bottle of brandy on the table as her contribution to the party; nobody would have wanted to be seen arriving empty-handed. She believed she would feel less alone with a drink in her hand. Once clutching a drink she would feel she fitted in and then would look for Austin.

An already inebriated doctor, who she half recognised from obstetrics, offered to make her a drink. He engaged, in some small talk then asked her if she had heard of the new research he was working on into transfer of pain from mother to father during childbirth. She acknowledged that it wasn't her field and she wasn't up to speed on the latest research. He then proceeded to tell her about a couple he was treating as he prepared her drink. Slowly, she became enthralled. The obstetrics doctor explained that at the start of childbirth he had transferred 10% of the pain from the mother to the husband. The husband coped well, so he had stepped it up and transferred 50% of the mother's pain. The husband seemed to be able to cope so he explained to Celia that he had bumped it right up to the dangerously high value of 90% and the husband still seemed to be able to cope. The outcome was that he delivered a pain-free, beautiful little baby girl to the couple. They were thrilled and everyone celebrated a terrific breakthrough for medical science. Celia congratulated him on his success.

Trouble was, he explained, when the couple arrived home they found the milkman dead on the front porch. The drinks doctor then guffawed and guffawed at his own joke and proceeded to spill half of Celia's drink all over the drinks table. He then spied her bottle of brandy amongst the 'raffle wine' and bottles of beer and poured himself a rather large one. Returning his blurred attention to her, he offered to make her another drink which she declined and after drying her glass, she turned, smiled at being caught out and laughed out loud at her gullibility. Then she made her way through the party throng.

In the garden she was delighted to come across some of the people to whom she had been introduced at the previous party with Austin. They welcomed her into their circle and presented her to those who she didn't know, one of whom was a larger than life American doctor on secondment to the UK. Also on his own, he immediately struck up a conversation with her. He was brash, he was overpowering and Celia felt the group were pleased he was giving all his attention to someone else. She felt she needed to take her turn at listening to him. He explained to Celia how important he was in the US and that his research work was of a critical nature. He was going to spend another two days in the UK, then was flying back to the US on a tour of prestigious conferences. Conferences usually only addressed by surgeons and consultants.

Celia yawned behind her hand. She suggested she ought to look for her partner but he insisted on joining her for another drink. At the drinks table which was now awash with spilled beer and wine, he poured her a larger than desired drink and also one for himself. She insisted she look for Austin. He insisted in turn on joining her, suggesting he didn't quite believe her. Comments about how he would never leave such a pretty lady at a party if he had invited her bounced off Celia but were becoming tedious.

After about an hour of fending him off she decided to head for the only place he couldn't come, the ladies. He said he would wait at the bottom of the stairs. There seemed no escape. After an inordinate time in the only loo in the house with people banging on the door to make sure nobody had died in there, she had to leave her sanctuary. If Austin wasn't there she would get a taxi and head for home.

Stepping off the bottom step of the stairs she looked furtively about and with a sigh couldn't see Dr America anywhere. She started back towards the group in the garden only to be confronted by Dr America who, with two or three more drinks inside him, looked like a sheep dog on heat.
Inherent brashness, alcohol and soon to leave the country made him very brave and despite her best efforts he clung to her like today's prize. Whilst he filled his glass once again Celia slipped back into the garden to her original friends. To her surprise several of the women apologised for dumping him on her and offered to look after her from now on. Celia asked one of the male doctors if he would just keep her company for a few minutes to get rid of Dr America. He agreed and slid his arm playfully around her waist and together they stood there joining in the conversation.

Dr America returned having sunk two more drinks. The conversation continued and the group moved about like chess pieces closing any gaps that would allow him to join in. Even with several drinks inside him it wasn't long before the situation became obvious and the mood suddenly changed.

Directed at the doctor with his arm around Celia's waist he said: "Hey buddy, that's my girl for tonight."

The doctor suggested in a very calm voice that 'much as he might like to think of them as buddies they were not! And this lady was certainly not his girl for the night'.

A huge push from Dr America as he elbowed his way into the circle sent the whole group sprawling in the garden, Celia included. Screams as women fell, the sound of broken glasses and shouts from the onlookers broke the party atmosphere. Dr America caught Celia by the arm as she was falling and said: "Honey, you and me are going to get out of this run-down joint and find a real party." Despite her protestations he started walking and pulling her towards the door into the house. The doctor who had offered her protection slipped between them and the house and suggested, very courteously, he let go of Celia.

"Or what limey?" growled the now, very unpleasant, Dr America.

Two quick steps forward and the doctor hit Dr America four times in amazingly quick succession. Bang, bang, bang, bang. Nobody saw the doctor's fists fly. The stunned big man went down on one knee letting go of Celia and trying to focus on the doctor who had hit him. He lumbered to stand up and once up, shook himself, gathered his wits and balance and focussed on the calm doctor standing in front of him. His big fists were clenched and he adopted a fighting pose. In again went the fearless doctor who hit him four more times, causing blood and mucus to fly everywhere from the American's nose. His eyes rolled in the top of his head and this time Dr America didn't get up.

The whole incident was over in seconds, the argument, the confrontation and the blows. A few of the partygoers carried the troublemaker through the house and into the front garden and called him a taxi.

Celia couldn't have been more grateful and was thanking the doctor profusely when she noticed his knuckles bleeding and beginning to swell. Quick as a flash she placed both his hands in ice buckets. Wincing with the initial pain he then relaxed as the ice worked its magic on the swelling and the grazes.

Behind her came a familiar voice: "Hey, I see you've made some friends." Austin chirped.

"Where the Hell have you been?"said Celia.

"That's the third time you've greeted me as if you really don't like me," replied Austin.

"It's not I don't like you, it's I don't like your time keeping," answered Celia.

One of the friends from the garden then took Austin quickly into the house to get him a drink and bring him up to speed about what had just happened before he put both feet in his mouth.

A little while later Celia and Austin sat together on a large sofa. The mood was tense. Austin had apologised a thousand times about not being able to leave a particularly interesting removal of a lung. With a torn dress courtesy of Dr America, Celia was no longer in a party mood and suggested they leave and get some food. Austin reluctantly agreed.

Another drink in a tiny Italian restaurant calmed the situation and they started to laugh about the evening, him tentatively and her laughter fuelled by alcohol. Two bottles of Chianti later and once again they had become friends.

***

Celia woke and decided not to open her eyes, not just yet. Her head hurt. Her head hurt a lot. She buried her head, eyes shut tight, into the pillow not wanting to wake. After some minutes she opened one eye and closed it immediately. This was not her pillow, this was not her bed! Those were not her curtains! Her mind painfully tried to recall the previous evening. It was all foggy. Then she sat up fearing the worst. Was she alone? She looked across to the other side of the bed. She was alone. She flopped back immediately regretting the sudden movement but with a huge sigh of relief.

But she wasn't thinking properly, did she still have her clothes on? Her hand shot below the covers and found all her clothes were intact. All her clothes, another huge sigh of relief. Ponderously she started to replay in her mind the events of the previous night. She remembered there had been a party. She remembered there had been a fight. Then she remembered that Austin had eventually turned up at the party. Piecing things together she recalled that they had gone to a restaurant together. She had drunk too much and regretted it deeply. Her head hurt really badly with a shooting pain at the back of her eyes. She closed them but it didn't help. Back to last night, she remembered that she and Austin had walked together for a while in the warm night air after the restaurant but then it became hazy. Street lights, front door, brandy. Her head hurt and now she needed water, lots of water.

A gentle knock at her door made her sit up in bed pulling the covers up to cover her modesty. Austin came in with a tray. The smell of strong coffee triggered a craving. Two boiled eggs and toast soldiers placed in the shape of a smile greeted her as he presented the tray to her. A large jug of water and two glasses were then brought in and put on the bedside table. Austin poured one for her and took one himself.

"God, you look awful," he said.

His tousled hair suggested all was not well with him either. He went on to say:

"And before you ask, the answer is no we didn't and that was because you all but passed out on me. Had you not passed out then, yes we probably would have."

"Thank you for looking after me... That is after the party!"

"I thought I had said sorry a thousand times for being late.'

Celia ignored him, drank a full glass of water, tucked into the eggs and soldiers then drank a full cup of the coffee before she spoke again.
"Have you got a spare tooth brush?"

"Of course. I keep a drawer full for ladies who pass out on me when I bring them back. However, I expect I can find one."

"And may I borrow one of your shirts please?"

Fifty minutes later and Celia emerged from the bathroom showered, hair washed, teeth cleaned only wearing one of Austin's linen shirts that swamped her. He in turn had shaved and dressed into sloppy clothes.
Celia, now feeling much more alive and in Austin's flat walked straight over to him and kissed him full on. When they separated she said: "Thank you."

"For what?"

"For what is about to happen!"

25 The Offer from Westerman's

Phase two of the UK Government trials was now complete and Carston and Jill were allowed a reluctant break. They went off in different directions. Married life returned to relative normality for Celia and Carston and for a few days they did couply things. They ate breakfast and dinner together and occasionally they met for lunch near the hospital. Secret yearnings dimmed for both of them and they again found themselves talking together and planning their future, post the big race. Celia had decided not to mention the party or staying over at Austin's flat to Carston. He wouldn't understand. In fact, she decided not to tell Carston anything about Austin at all. Life was virtually normal again and any discussion about the party would surely destabilise their marriage.

Then one evening at about 10.30pm when they were just about to go to bed there was a knock at the door. Both looked at each other quizzically. Visitors were rare.

Carston cautiously opened the door to a man who introduced himself as Pickard.

Pickard wished to speak to Dr Carston Prestwick, alone. In the quick introduction Carston deduced Pickard to be a military man from his upright stance, neat appearance and handshake. Carston showed him into the sitting room and offered him a drink. Whisky was agreed upon for both.

Pickard explained that he worked for Westerman's Railway Company and he was here to see if Dr Prestwick would be interested in joining them. Carston was flattered but thanked Pickard saying he was fully committed to Rosser's. Regardless of Carston's comment Pickard continued. The offer would be a place on Westerman's board of directors and a golden hello. The only condition was that he would have to make the decision within two days and join the company, bringing with him all his research.

Carston listened intently, so did Celia from behind the, slightly ajar, bedroom door. Being a shrewd negotiator and a Scot, Carston asked for more information. Pickard obliged. The offer was to add 50% to Carston's current salary and the golden hello would be for £5,000 when he signed.

Arguments for and against flew through Carston's mind.

The UK Government wouldn't be particularly bothered if he switched railway companies as they weren't bothered who was doing the steam trials for them. In fact for it to be shared between two organisations would offset some of the criticism currently being levelled at their favouritism towards Rosser's.

On the other hand, Rosser's had been very good to him. They had paid for him to go to university, paid for his masters and paid for his doctorate. He felt he owed them.

No, he would stay with Rosser's.

Carston turned to Pickard and said 'no thank you' to his generous offer.

Pickard thought for a moment then suggested the golden hello could be raised to take in the special circumstances of a very quick decision, say to £15,000 and then he stayed silent while Carston digested the potential massive windfall.

Celia couldn't believe her ears. £15,000 would buy a detached house, outside London. It would set them up for life. Surely he wouldn't turn it down. She wanted to burst in to the sitting room and shout of course he'll take it.

Carston thanked Pickard and said he would be in touch the next day and showed him the door. Celia burst into the hallway and threw her arms around her neck.

"What's all this for?"

"£15,000, it's like winning the pools."

"I thought the conversation was supposed to be private."

"It was. It was just between the three of us."

"Well, don't get too excited. I may not take it."

"What?'

"I may not take it."

"You mean you would turn down £15,000 and a seat on the board of directors?"

"That's exactly what I mean. Rosser's have been very good to me and that would be a real slap in the eye for them. They would rightly think twice about investing in anybody else ever again. I'll sleep on it."

Dumbstruck Celia watched him go off to bed.

The next day Carston talked the offer over the phone with Jill. She listened intently and asked what was it that Rosser's had offered him in comparison with the

Westerman offer? Rosser's had, apart from the golden hello, inferred he would be on the board within two years where his salary would be significantly increased. After some deliberation it was Jill who pointed out that there were only a very few organisations like Westerman's that would have had the money or the nerve to pull off the train hi-jacking. After the call with Jill, Carston didn't need to think for very long. He turned the offer from Westerman's down flat.

When he told Celia she was beside herself. That evening they hardly spoke and she went to bed early in a huff. At 10.30pm again there was a knock at the door. Carston answered. Pickard was invited into the sitting room again. Celia positioned herself strategically behind the bedroom door.

This time Pickard said he understood Dr Prestwick's position and that Rosser's had indeed been good to him paying for all his education and offering him a director's position at the end of it. Perhaps there was a halfway house. This time Pickard offered not for Carston to join Westerman's but to throw the railway steam race that was not so very far away. The 30th April. Carston listened dispassionately. The purse for throwing the race was the same as the golden hello. £15,000. All he had to do was to ensure that Westerman's won the race and the money would be his.

Carston thanked him for his offer and told him he would let him know the following day. Of course

Pickard said that if he disclosed either meeting they would be denied and Westerman's would do everything in their power to discredit him. Following that, not so veiled threat, Carston showed him the door after flatly turning down the offer again.

"You can't be serious," shouted Celia. "You're going to turn down £15,000 for coming second in a stupid old train race."

"Yes."

"You must be mad."

"Who's to say they will pay if I did throw the race? Who would I complain to if I threw the race and they didn't pay? Their   chairman? No.   They are shifty, underhand and maybe, just maybe were behind the train hi-jacking when Percy was killed."

A slightly more conciliatory Celia took herself off to bed.

26
The Beans are Spilled

As crackers of the music box code, Carston and Celia maintained an interest in what was happening in Hucknall but were reminded this was Government business and to keep well away from the site on the 1st March.

The Government plan was that the whole of Hucknall was to be locked down but in secret. At night on the day before the demonstration 30 truckloads of British soldiers were driven into the site, who secreted themselves everywhere. Some dug themselves into camouflaged foxholes; some dressed as workmen and others as guests. The area of demonstration was heavily guarded and the route for the aero engines carefully checked.

The order of proceedings was such: The aero engines were to be set up for close examination by the European visitors and the finale was to be a demonstration of one of the engines that had been installed in a newly designed plane. The plane was to give a flying demonstration whilst the visitors looked on. From the site's position everything was set up as planned.

Liaison between Government departments discussed the fact that an attempt was to be made on the visitors' lives and on the latest aeroplane. Contingences were put in place but it was imperative that the whole cell planning the bombing was all caught.

As the day approached the cell members were also ready. Their plan was to drive their stolen army truck loaded with explosives in through a back gate along with the engines and just leave it close to the demonstration and visitors. A timed fuse would allow the perpetrators to escape and observe the destruction from a considerable distance. All was going according to plan for Hawk.

Major Brown decided to drive up and see for himself what was so important about the information the Hawk had wanted from him and if there were any consequences to his action. Again he drove to the Seven Stars pub in Hucknall, but was told by a soldier outside that unless his business was urgent he was to leave the area immediately. Not wanting to draw any attention to himself he drove out of Hucknall and into the next village, Linby. There he settled into a small pub and chatted to the landlord who was busier than usual a consequence of every pub in Hucknall being shut. Apparently he'd heard that everyone was allowed to go about their normal business in Hucknall but something was happening which he didn't quite understand.

When all the European visitors had been settled and the Government demonstration was well under way, the bogus truck loaded not with aero engine parts but with high explosives with all its paperwork intact, drove through the gates and into the compound. The truck was directed to the same area as the other engines. The driver and his passenger then proceeded to set the charge and abandon their vehicle.

Immediately the bombers were outside the vehicle they were surrounded by troops who rose up from foxholes and from every conceivable building. There was no escape and the bomb disposal team quickly moved in. The exhibition continued without incident and the new Spitfire aeroplane flew a perfect maiden flight.

At 6pm Major Brown drove back into Hucknall and to the Seven Stars pub. He sat in the corner and started a conversation with two old colliers who were happy to be bought beer. When the major inquired about the ex-RSM one of the old colliers bluntly told him: "Blew his brains out the other day." And with that he pushed the local paper towards the major. There on the front page was a photo and a brief account of the ex-RSM's confession. The major went cold.

"The bastard's been selling info to the enemy. Spilled all the beans to the red caps and then went and shot his self! Dying's too good for him. Should have been thrown down the colliery shaft, along with thems he sold it to, the bastards."

The major drank up and left wondering what 'beans' had exactly been spilled.

27
Race Ready

Sadly Celia couldn't get the time off to go and watch the big race but as Carston pointed out it could be five days before all the competitors had run and the result was known. He explained that all the competitors had to wait at the same hotel for the race order to be announced, then they could go to their trains.

He explained in detail to her that this year there were five competing railway companies. A newcomer to the race called Bonehill and Co., Caterpillar and Cummings with their steam and diesel engine, highly contested by the purists of the race, a Scottish Highland company, Westerman's and finally Rosser's. Each had a slot when they would attempt their speed trial which was drawn out of a hat. Each complete train was to be kept well away from the other competitors and thoroughly checked by the judges.

Carston thought he might stay with the Rosser's driver and fireman and sleep on the train until the race was over. Especially after Percy's death, he wasn't taking any chances. The rules were very strict and judges had already inspected the track.

Celia told him she couldn't wait till he had won the race and was back home to celebrate and look for a house in the country.

There was not one nut or bolt that hadn't been taken off polished and refitted by Carston's team. The engine fairly shone. He couldn't have been more proud. Even Nigel the Chairman of Rosser's walked around the fine engine and carriages and seeing a dull area on one of the carriage doors, removed his handkerchief from his suit pocket and proceeded to polish it till it shone. The series 6 locomotive that Carston had been given was a two-year-old engine with a proven track record for speed. Carston and his team had installed not only the smoke diffuser, but also the modifications he had now been working on for three years through university and in the UK Government depot. Their own trials on this engine had been very encouraging but like all engineers he wanted just another month to perfect it.

Jill had asked to be relieved of her duties with the UK Government trials to observe first-hand the possibilities of Carston's commercial modifications being adopted UK-wide. She was allowed to go as long as she did not participate in the race. This was fine for her for she believed this race to be Carston's race.

Every wheel had been taken off its axle, balanced and skimmed for perfect running, every bearing had been run-in independently, refitted and filled with grease ready for the race. Even the coal had been especially selected and mixed for the day. A special trainload had been purchased for the race. Two collieries had been selected. One from the western side of the anthracite fields in South Wales and one from the Rhondda Valley. Not only had the colliery been chosen but even the seam. Half the coal came from the Stanllyd anthracite seam mined 300 yards below ground in Cwmgwilli Colliery. Men lying on their sides in the three-foot seam had filled the coal into special trams ready for transportation to the Rosser's depot. And the other half was bright steam coal from the Big Vein seam on the eastern side of the coalfield. Combined, the coal had a unique calorific value, low sulphur, very low ash and little moisture content.

The carriages, seven in all, had been inspected to ensure they conformed with the rules. There was now nothing left to do but wait for the day and hope all went well. George, the driver on the loco that had been 'doctored' to crash on the night of Carston's honeymoon had now recovered from the loss of Percy, but there were grave reservations by Rosser's management team that he would hang together for the most stressful race of his life. It was Carston who insisted upon using him, to the point of saying that if George doesn't drive then he wouldn't go either. His faith filled George with pride. George had quietly said to Carston: "I won't let you down sir, I really won't."

"I know, I know."

The only thing George insisted upon was that a small plaque be put in the cab for Percy. He had paid for it himself and had it inscribed. He fitted it himself. It read...

In Memory
of
Percy Brown
The Best Fireman
Ever

When it was polished and shone like gold he stood back and quietly said to Carston: "It will be good to have Percy along, sir."

Carston agreed.

Now they were ready.

28 The Redirected Taxi

Whenever Carston was going to be away for a while, Celia moved into the Nurses' Home near the hospital. She said that it was easier for her to work late in the evenings and she didn't like coming home to an empty flat along the dark streets on her own. Carston completely understood. They both packed independently for the next few days, kissed, and told one another they loved and would miss each other. Celia waved, wished him good luck and jumped into the waiting taxi.

She shouted to the taxi driver:" The Hospital Nurses' Home please," but when she was around the corner she changed the instruction to Austin's flat.

This was her routine when Carston was away and she felt guilty for a while but the sweet anticipation of the clandestine meeting was a powerful one. In contrast to Carston, when she was staying at Austin's flat she couldn't wait for him to arrive, she willed the minutes to hurry past. She kept moving the curtains to see if he was coming. While she waited for him she cleaned his flat. It wasn't a chore, she wanted to look after him, and he always noticed.

She and Austin spoke the same language. His Scottish accent was like coming home it was so familiar and reminded her of all the good things she'd left behind. They used words from home that no-one else understood and laughed about the confusion it caused. She put flowers on the table for their meal and he noticed! When he came home she didn't kiss him on the cheek and ask about his day, she flung her arms around his neck and kissed him for all she was worth and he kissed her back. She felt he couldn't wait to be with her either.

In the mornings she lay alongside him combing his jet black, unruly hair from his eyes and stroking his bushy eyebrows. She ran her fingers through the black, bear hair that covered his whole body, teasing till he couldn't stand it any longer and then stopped abruptly, turned away playing hard to get. When she woke feeling frisky Celia wouldn't take no for an answer. She tumbled all over him letting her lithe body arouse him until his body signalled he was very awake although his eyes were shut tight, feigning sleep.

On one occasion she had been preparing their evening meal when he came home unexpectedly early. Still in a pinny he came into the kitchen, lifted her off the ground and took her squealing with delight into the bedroom where they made love as passionately as she had ever imagined in her wildest and raunchiest school-girl dreams. The meal was ruined, the saucepans were burned but it didn't matter. What mattered was the closeness, what mattered was they wanted each other so much, what mattered was they had fallen in love. When they made love, it was with such passion, she cried.

But one day she bounced into his flat but could immediately tell things were different. This time he did only kiss her on the cheek, and once she had thrown her bags into the bedroom he asked her to come and sit down and talk to him. She knew before he said a word the wonderful lovemaking days were over, she knew this was to be the 'no commitment conversation', she felt empty, she missed him already and the tears started to run before he had chance to say a word.

Austin explained he had been offered an amazing opportunity in the hospital at Fort William as a fully qualified doctor. What he went on to say completely threw her. They were also looking for a qualified paediatrician to join their team. He told her he had fallen completely in love with her and despite this offer coming far too soon for either of them, he wanted her to come with him. He wanted her to leave

Carston and move to Fort William. There they would set up home together and live back in Scotland.

All was silent between them. That silence that meant scenarios were flashing through both their minds. Amazing scenes of what life could be like, of children living by the sea, of picnics on the shores of lochs together as a family. Of wanting to be with someone and build a future together so much. Against this were the dark scenes of destruction, a life hardly started to be built between two people shattered, of tears, of recriminations, of guilt.

Reality and fantasy were clashing in her mind like Titans. Reality of, 'too soon, hardly know each other and huge risk' and fantasy of, 'if you don't do it now you will regret it forever and, you already know the answer don't you.'

He started to speak but she shushed him. She told him she loved him more than anyone in the world but she had decided she couldn't go with him. Carston andher hadn't given their marriage a chance and it wasn't fair. Austin's idea, magical as she believed they would make it, wasn't fair on any of them. Carston hadn't done anything wrong except work incredibly hard towards this big race and for the Government. She, in turn, needed another three years in London to make her name in paediatrics. He must take the opportunity and go on his own with her blessing.

She ended by saying that even if they did go together she felt he would be held back in the tiny village mentality of narrow-minded thinking that they would encounter in every Fort William shop, kirk, hospital, school, in fact everywhere.

They made love that night to say goodbye. They made love that night to say they loved each other but accepted that what they wanted just couldn't be.

That night after they made love they both cried.

29
Elated, Gutted, Celebrated

Three trains had run their race, two to go. The first train, the Highland train had achieved a very acceptable time on both runs and the crews could be very proud of their little engine against such powerful adversaries. The actual time wasn't known except by the train crew who took their own times, times not accepted by the judges. The second train, Bonehill and co. had blown a hole, the size of a dustbin lid, in its boiler and had to be been towed to a siding and the third, half steam, half diesel, had beaten the previous best speed record and the team were sitting back smugly in the hotel despite the barrage of criticism from Westerman's.

Rosser's was next. Their train overnight had been driven to the sidings above the race start and Carston and George had opted to stay with it, just in case. The team had fired her up in the morning and they made their apprehensive way to the starting place. The judges inspected the train inside and out and once satisfied, waved the train off. The day was a fine April day and there was no rain. The sun broke through the wispy clouds giving the day a positive aura for them. Winning would mean so much to Carston and George occasionally found him gazing out of the cab in a far off way before the race. George realised that the credibility of all Carston's five years' research work rested on this race.

Jill had wanted to come to be part of the race but as with ships, women were seen to be unlucky and the last thing she wanted to bring him was anything but good luck. After several whiskies late one night before the race, Carston had confided in Jill that his wife didn't know one end of a steam engine from another and yawned whenever he mentioned what he was doing. He told Jill that Celia had found it difficult to become excited when he mentioned the race. Carston stopped abruptly at that, feeling he was about to say things that probably were best left unsaid. However, Carston would have loved for Jill to be with them in the race.

The first few miles before the race the big engine loped along with no effort whatsoever. As it reached the start line its speed was at 100 mph, the last steam speed record. The big engine just kept going and going up in speed. It reached 126 mph and George suggested this had smashed the record but the same speed would be required on the return journey. They

186

held it at 126 mph for the requisite time and allowed the big engine to slow down over a long distance.

After the finish line there was a long tedious turn around for the train through the countryside before they could start on the same track for the return journey.

As they hit the start line on the return journey they were travelling at 115mph and the big engine was powering up to 126mph. George grinned at Carston and went to the back of the cab and gave Percy's plaque a polish.

Then all Hell broke loose. Red flags were waving at them from every bridge and every crossing. A red flag meant a serious problem for which the locomotive was forced to stop. At this time they didn't know if there was a problem with their train that they couldn't see or there was a problem with the track, but the warning had to be taken with the greatest seriousness. George started the engine slow down. He glanced up at the speed just before he started the slow down, 130 mph.

Four miles on and chugging at a speed now of 20 mph they came to a bridge and heard a race steward shout that there had been two old bicycles thrown onto the track up ahead. The bicycles had been cleared from the track by the time George and Carston arrived at the site and green flags waved them through.

Carston was devastated. Their recorded speed could not be entered as a record as it was only one way. George and Carston calculated the rest of the run and decided there wasn't the distance to reach even 100mph let alone the 126mph required to win.

In silence, the two of them cruised to the finish line in silence at about 60mph.

***

The announcement of the steam race winner was to be made at the final dinner.

Carston, the Chairman of Rosser's and four directors sat at their table and, being English sportsmen, were magnanimous in their pending defeat. Westerman's table was raucous and Major Brown was passing the port for the third time to Pickard, who had hardly acknowledged Carston when the Race Chairman's gavel hit the table.

He presented a brand new prize to the Highland Railway Company for their performance and suggested the other contestants should beware of the little guy, for next year they could well take the top prize.

The Race Chairman then commiserated with Bonehill's team jokingly suggesting that there was a siding not far from the hotel where there were a considerable number of spares going cheap. His joke was taken in the spirit of the evening, as they all knew their engines were at full stretch and the same could have happened to them, at any time.

The diesel/steam railway company was ruled out of order for the technicality of not informing the judges beforehand of their dual power arrangements, to which the whole table rose as one and left the room to the jeers and whistles from Westerman's.

That left two, Rosser's and Westerman's.

The Race Chairman read out the impressive speeds that had been achieved by both engine crews. Carston could not believe that Westerman's had achieved a similar speed to his on either of the runs. He was devastated. He concluded they must have doctored the results, they must have bribed the officials, they must have swapped engines, there must be a mistake. Then the realisation dawned on him that he wasn't the only person in the world doing research on locomotive speeds. They could also have had a breakthrough. Carston's heart sank.

Major Brown smugly waved over to the Chairman of Rosser's. The Chairman of Rosser's reluctantly acknowledged the gesture.

The Race Chairman then continued explaining to the audience that as Rosser's return trip had to be aborted due to deleterious material on the track (guffaws from the Westerman's table) the judges could not take the run into consideration and therefore Rosser's were disqualified.

A roar rose from the Westerman's table.

The 1st prize was awarded to Westerman's.

Just as the Rosser's table had expected, the catcalls and cheering from Westerman's table was deafening. The Rosser's team politely clapped, congratulated the Westerman's team and made their soulful way out of the dining room to the bar. Carston stayed a fitting length of time with the Rosser's Directors and then made his dejected way to bed.

The Westerman's team then hit the bar hard.

Around 20minutes later Carston thought he heard a knock at the door. He listened again and despite the cheering and celebrations still going on downstairs, he heard the faint knocking at his door again. He quietly opened it and there stood Jill and George who slipped into his room uninvited.

We think you should come with us they whispered. Carston dutifully dressed and, after checking nobody was about, followed the pair out of the hotel and into the night. A car was waiting for them and they drove to a siding where the Westerman's train was parked. With a small torch George led the way. He went into the garage and shushed Carston and Jill as there were still Westerman's staff about.

Jill and George undid one of the side panels on the big Westerman race engine and there to Carston's amazement was an identical set of modifications he had been working on for the last four years. Carston kept looking at Jill then George then back to the engine. They heard a member of Westerman's staff walking towards them but as Major Brown had sent a barrel of beer and a crate of whisky for the crew, few of the Westerman staff even knew what day it was. The man came close to where they were hiding, undid his trousers, had a pee and returned unsteadily to the party.

All Carston could say under his breath was: "The bastards, the bastards used my modifications they couldn't have done it any other way."

The trio returned to the hotel and woke all the race judges including the Race Chairman who followed Carston, Jill and George back by car to the Westerman sidings and after a thorough examination of the engine the judges declared the race null and void and returned to the hotel. By this time most of the Westerman's table were albeit unconscious and an announcement could wait for the morning.

George and Jill returned to their hotel next door where the less senior members of the management teams were staying and Carston went to bed perplexed as to how Westerman's had acquired his modifications, but pleased he had solved the puzzle.

Again there was a faint knocking on his bedroom door. This time it was just Jill. She slid quietly into his room. There was no need for anything to be said about the race. Now they both knew. There was no need for anything to be said about the last six months of working together. They both knew.

Without saying anything she produced a bottle of champagne, opened it, poured two glasses and stood right in front of him just like the night she couldn't get home because of the fog. They sipped the champagne and all he said was: I've waited for a moment like this to be with you, any moment would have done but today, tonight, this moment is very special."

They sipped and kissed and hugged as they celebrated. They toasted George and Percy and then made up for all the wasted evenings they had missed. They spent the night together as close as two people could possibly be, excited by the thoughts of the future and exhausted by the last six months at the same time. They congratulated themselves to the bottom of the bottle. They slept very little that night but lay in each other's arms, allowing the champagne to speak for them and say the things that until then had remained unsaid.

Neither believed the race was really over.

They rose early to breakfast with the judges and Nigel the Rosser's Chairman, who was now over the moon with the news.

Throughout the night the steam race judges had informed the Government who had impounded the

Westerman's train and arrested a bogus engineer who had worked for Rosser's.

It transpired that the bogus engineer who worked on the Rosser's race engine had at one time worked for Westerman's and was still on that company's payroll. It was he who had been making the secret drawings and taking photographs at night. It was he who had nearly been caught after which Carston and Jill had to destroy any copies of documents or drawings. Then it had been too late, the damage had been done and the engineer stayed at Rosser's in case there was any more information required by Westerman's.

When the judges made the announcement at breakfast there was silence. A silence immediately followed by a group of Government officials asking the heavily hung-over Westerman's team to accompany them to London.

Jill and Carston looked on as the forlorn band was led out. George was waiting at the door watching the proceedings. Suddenly he stepped forward and tapped Pickard on the shoulder. Pickard turned. George said: "Percy sends his regards." Pickard didn't understand and shook his head to clear it but George's right fist connected with Pickard's face and jogged his memory. Pickard stumbled backwards and broke a table and chair in his fall. Two burly policemen then helped the unconscious Pickard out to the Black Maria.

Eventually, George explained to Carston and Jill that he had recognised Pickard from the night Percy was killed and then he discovered Pickard was in the Westerman's team so George had informed the local police. Together the police and George had informally agreed on just one hit. George had made it count for Percy.

George, Nigel the Chairman and the team travelled back to London in the Rosser's train and Carston and Jill stayed on for another three days to sort out any paperwork, but really it was a gift from the Chairman.

On the second day whilst out walking together, Jill asked Carston what he was going to do next as she was returning to be with her father and wanted him to come too. Carston knew this would be Jill's eventual outcome but had hoped they would be able to stay together for a few more months to finish all of the work.

They walked for a while until Carston broke the silence. He asked if she wanted the engineer to return with her or the man? There wasn't a moment's hesitation. She replied: "I want my husband-to-be to return with me."

They walked and talked during the remaining day about the future. The offer to Carston was so tempting; to be with the person he had so wanted to have met in the first place. But, this was not fair on Celia. Although she had no interest in steam, he had loved her for herself and ever since their marriage he had been away from her. Their brief marriage hadn't stood a chance. Only six months ago he thought he had found the one he wanted to stay with forever and it was circumstances that had driven a wedge between them. He still hadn't even met her family.

He told Jill he had decided to stay with Celia.

They said their goodbyes over dinner, they said their goodbyes in bed, they said their goodbyes over breakfast and every time he said goodbye he wondered if this would be a decision he would regret for the rest of his life.

Jill left on her way to re-join her father and Carston's world felt empty.

But his decision had been made. He would try to make amends with Celia and build what, until quite recently, he believed could be a happy marriage.
He bought two first class tickets to Paris, a bottle of champagne and made his way home. This was to be the start of their future where things needed to be put back in perspective. He was a little apprehensive of his reception.

Celia was at home preparing dinner for the two of them. This was also to be her bid for the future and she had chosen her future to be with him. She also had champagne on ice and candles had been lit on the dining room table and all around the room.

When he arrived home they celebrated the outcome of the race. She noticed Carston seemed a touch quiet as if waiting for the right moment for something and he went off to get changed out of his work clothes. As she waited for him to return to the kitchen she found herself watching the bubbles in her champagne glass make their way to the top of the flute, pop and fizz showering her hand with the finest of spray. If she concentrated very hard she could just feel the spray tingling on the fine hairs of her fingers that held the glass. If she held the glass close to her nose she could feel the bubbles popping. In this tense moment she was concentrating on the things closest to her. The tiny champagne spray made her smile.

They walked together into the dining room and there, on his place setting, as a surprise for him, was his music box. He was delighted and it was then for the first time he noticed she was wearing his pendant. He lifted the lid of the music box and it played Edelweiss. He smiled at her knowingly; apparently the police had rounded up the owner of the antiques shop, Hans, the weasel man, Hawk and Major Brown. That afternoon they had returned all the stolen articles to Celia including Carston's cherished pen.

With the candles flickering all around them in the tiny dining room and his favourite tune playing, Carston suddenly dropped onto one knee in front of her, held her hand and asked if she would marry him all over again. Not the ceremony bit, not the reception bit or his father getting drunk bit, but the just the two of them bit. She cried, immediately accepting.

Then he passed her the tickets, the first class tickets to Paris. She flung her arms around his neck in thank you; the only proviso from her was that they travel by ship or car or bicycle or pram, but not by train.

They both laughed.

30 Who'd Have Thought It?

Two years on and Celia was living in her dream house with wisteria hanging over the porch to the front door; the delighted mother of two beautiful, red-haired little girls. She was living happily near Fort William with her husband, the newly appointed senior consultant, Mr Austin McGregor. Two years on and Dr Carston L.G. Prestwick and Professor Jill Hollingsworth were working on the prestigious East/West railway to Beijing. Carston and Jill were now the proudest parents of one handsome son and one, very pretty daughter.

The End